BLESSED

are the

PEACEMAKERS

A NOVEL BY
RUSSELL M. CHACE

TUKONA BOOKS LLC
P.O. Box 447; Cañon City, CO 81215

TRADE PAPERBACK ISBN: 978-1-733037-16-7

E-BOOK ISBN: 978-1-733037-17-4

PRINTED IN THE UNITED STATES.

10 9 8 7 6 5 4 3 2

TAKONA BOOKS, LLC
COLORADO

DEDICATION

*To my church family in
Two Rivers, Alaska.*

Those were the days.

PROLOGUE

Caleb Moore gazed at the stout log cabin from the top of the low rise. Two Buffalo Soldiers, carrying military payroll through Oklahoma Indian Territory, were barricaded inside.

Caleb felt a sneer cross his face as an idea crossed his mind. "I'll fix their bacon. You boys, get that wagon by the coral there and load it with hay and bring it up here. The rest of you, keep firing. Give 'em cover."

Soon, the wagon arrived.

"Line it up to the cabin door."

Caleb tied the tongue back and the front axle fast to the body so it wouldn't veer off course. "This should smoke 'em out."

Digging in his vest pocket, he produced a Lucifer. This, he struck on a wagon iron, produced a flame, and then set the hay on fire.

"When they come out, don't kill 'em, just let 'em run. All we want is the money in the payroll box. Got it?"

Everyone nodded and murmured their approval.

"Good. Giv'er a shove, boys!"

The wagon began to roll, slowly at first but soon picked up speed. By the time the wagon reached the cabin, it was a roaring blaze. The impact smashed the door open and scattered fire into the cabin as well as on the roof and along the front wall.

Caleb waited. "Why don't they come out, the fools?"

The cabin walls quickly flamed up, and soon the front of the cabin and roof was a roaring inferno—the likes of which you seldom see.

He heard hideous screaming and wailing coming from inside the cabin. His heart leaped to his throat.

That was not what he expected at all.

He watched in horror as two figures crawled out from under the burning wagon. Their clothes and hair were on fire.

The gang, in their blood lust, and, perhaps mercifully, opened fire. One flaming figure stood up and stumbled toward the water trough. The other continued to crawl a few more feet before collapsing.

The cabin burnt to the ground, the money was destroyed, and the outlaws walked away with nothing.

C oy Tucker stood at the second-floor cabin deck railing of the stern wheeler *St. Michael* as it nosed into the Yukon riverbank at Rampart in the territory of Alaska. A leaden gray, drizzly sky reflected his mood as a chilled fall breeze wafted down his neck. Living most of his life on the western frontier, the Alaskan frontier was a big change from what he was used to. Coy pulled his collar up against the cold.

It was late September. There had been talk amongst the passengers about a gold strike made here in '94. John Minook, a Russian and Athabaskan half-breed, they said, pulled some good pay out of a hole up on the creeks behind the trading post.

Most of the passengers, however, wanted to push on to Dawson. It was still more than nine hundred miles to the Klondike, and they ran a risk of the boat freezing in the Yukon River ice before reaching their goal. If that happened, the boat would be their home for seven months until the ice melted and set them free. Most passengers elected to push on, driven by their lust for Klondike gold and fear of missing out on staking the good claims.

Coy was a cautious man. Besides, he wasn't there for the gold.

He reached down, grabbed his duffel bag, and slung it over his left shoulder. He wanted his right arm free because, well, you just never know. Turning a little to his left, he eased his way down the narrow stairway to the main deck. There, he joined Frank Canton, George MacGowan, John Powell, and a few others who had elected to stay as well, and waited for the gangplank to be lowered.

It seemed all the inhabitants of Rampart turned out to witness the arrival of the stern wheeler—evidently curious of who was on board and, more importantly, if any supplies were being offloaded.

There would be disappointment about the latter, for the *St Michael* was a small ship bought from a Jesuit mission by a hastily formed company led by E.T. Barnette to move their freight to Dawson. It was manned by an inept crew. Coy was mildly amazed they had made it that far.

A man accustomed to vigilance, Coy quickly scanned the waterfront scene. The village of Rampart sat on the third bench above water level. A virgin forest of tall white spruce, paper birch, and a few other deciduous tree species surrounded the hastily carved-out-of-the-wilderness settlement.

A well-worn path led up to the trading post, evidently Rampart's center of activity. Bearded men in coveralls, mackinaws, and hats milled about in groups on the three benches, hands in their pockets. One man's arm hung in a sling. A few women lingered here and there amongst the men.

As he made his way down the gangplank and up the path toward the trading post, Coy noticed one individual, a shorter man, who stood alone on the boardwalk.

He was dressed in black pants, a black vest with a gold pocket watch chain over a gray wool shirt, and a white tie. His attire was topped off with a black derby hat and a black coat.

Getting closer, Coy saw he sported a thick white mustache and piercing gray eyes—the kind of eyes that seemed to cut right through the tough exterior of a man to search his inner soul.

Coy set his duffel bag on the boardwalk and leaned it against the building. Looking northeast along the upper bench, Coy saw something he had seen many times in many other mining camps—a row of hastily built log cabins and white canvas tents.

In front of the dwellings lay the remains of limbs, bark, and wood chips in scattered profusion. The sounds of saws, hammers, and axes accentuated the sense of urgency to get shelters made before the long, cold, dark winter nights descended over the land. Here and there, a stump protruded through the debris.

"You ain't like the others."

Coy turned toward the voice. It was the shorter man in the black derby hat. Looking into his gray eyes, Coy saw years of hard work and harsh winters. A quick smile crossed the man's face, and he stuck his hand out.

"I'm Captain Al Mayo. Most people call me Cap. I own the trading post here. I'm also the mayor of Rampart."

Being on the river for as long as Coy had been, he'd heard the name mentioned with respect in circles of polite conversation. Cap appeared to be friendly, but cautious, and one to get right to the point with no idle chit-chat. Coy decided he liked him.

He took Cap's hand and shook it. Cap Mayo had a vice-like grip.

"Coy Tucker's the name. Been around a while I take it?"

A smile crossed Cap's face.

"Son, I don't mind sayin' I'm a squaw-man, and I been here ever since the Yukon was a little creek and Chilkoot Pass was a hole in the ground."

Coy felt the slight curl of a smile. "So, what makes you think I'm not like the others?"

Cap hesitated a moment. He looked Coy up and down. "You're alert. You spotted me right off. You're cautious. By your grip and the small scars on your hand, you've done some hard work. But your hands are soft. You haven't done much physical labor lately. By the bulges on your hips under your long black coat, I'd say you're packin' iron. You're not here to *dig* gold, are you?"

Coy was mildly surprised. Obviously, Cap Mayo was observant as well. Coy didn't think the two *Colt Peacemakers* showed under his coat... and what did Cap mean by '*dig*' gold? The implication, Coy decided, was maybe Cap thought Coy was there for the gold, but not necessarily by digging it up. Scenes of his misspent youth flitted through his mind and Coy Tucker mentally pushed them down into the dark recesses of his brain. At one time, that would have been a correct assumption.

Did Cap know who and what I'd been? Coy wondered.

"Sounds like you got me figured out... almost. I'm an itinerant preacher. I want to start a church in your community."

Cap frowned. "Not another Jesuit or Episcopalian missionary? We got a lot of 'em up and down the river. A more pompous passel of people I've never met."

"Yes, you do, and no, I am not. I'm a Baptist by conviction."

Cap looked down at the boardwalk for a few seconds as if pondering the situation. Then, looking at Coy said, "So what's with the irons? The other preachers don't pack heat. Ain't you supposed to be meek and mild?"

Coy took a breath and slowly exhaled.

"I don't recall anything in the scriptures that says a man can't protect himself or others. In fact, the scriptures say a man is worse than an infidel if he does not provide for his own. That includes safety and security. Abraham killed a bunch of bad guys to rescue his nephew, Lot and his family. Jesus himself made and used a whip to drive the corrupt moneylenders and loan sharks out of the temple.

"There are many other examples in the Bible. A gun or a sword or a shovel is only a tool. A tool is only as good as the man using it. It can be used for evil, and it can be used to stop evil.

"Yes, I believe in peace and getting along with others. I want that more than anything. But sometimes, a man's gotta stand up for those oppressed. And, if it takes a gun to do it, then so be it."

Cap Mayo's eyes grew a little wider as he peered at Coy.

"Like I said, you ain't like the others." Another quick smile crossed his face. "Now, if you'll excuse me, I got customers to take care of."

Coy Tucker watched Cap disappear into the trading post, then glanced down to the water's edge. The *St. Michael* gently lowered a ton of supplies, dangling from the yard boom's cable onto the beach. He and the other passengers who disembarked had made prior arrangements with Captain Barnette of the *St. Michael* to off-load their supplies.

Coy didn't have the full ton most prospectors carried, because he lacked the picks, shovels, and other mining tools. His outfit consisted of a larger tent to use for meetings, along with a wood stove, clothing, sleeping gear, and the normal foodstuffs like flour, bacon, beans, sugar, coffee, and tea.

Another unique supply he brought was evaporated vegetables—a hundred pounds worth, said to be made especially for the Klondike trade. They were a tad tasteless but added variety to the wild-game stews. Besides, they supposedly retained some vitamins touted to ward off scurvy.

Coy wasn't concerned with theft and decided his provisions were fine where they sat. In the Northland, theft of a man's food supply was dealt with by flogging the accused and then releasing them on a raft down the Yukon to an uncertain end—usually carried out by a quick miners' meeting.

Behind the cabins and the trader's store, rose another bench of land still covered in spruce and birch trees. Coy shouldered his duffel, then hiked up and chose a spot of his own.

After staking out his plot of land, he left his duffel to mark the spot and made his way to the trader's store to have it recorded. Since Cap was the mayor, all the mining camp business and miners' meetings were conducted at his trading post.

Some prospectors had come in from the creeks celebrating their good fortune. The *cheechakoes* from the *St. Michael* hung on every word they spoke. There was an over-all noisy din of laughter and talk.

"There! All done," Cap said in a raised voice as he finished penciling in Coy's boundary lines. "Just be aware we may have to adjust them later if we have to lay out a street and other lots later."

Coy's attention was suddenly arrested by something seeping through his subconscious. Was it the turn of a phrase or the tone in which it was said? Coy did not know. Turning his head, he saw a large man shove an Indian girl aside.

"Outta my way, Klootch. I need some tur-backy."

The Indian girl stumbled against the counter, dropping the packages she held onto the floor.

Coy tightened his jaw and pushed his way through the crowd.

Standing behind the big man, Coy took his Bible out of his coat pocket and held it over his heart with his left hand.

"I believe you owe the lady an apology."

The miners on each side of the big man turned, looked at Coy, and backed away.

The noise in the room subsided.

The big man turned with a slight limp and looked Coy up and down. His eyes rested on the Bible, and then he looked into Coy's eyes.

"Pardon me?"

"Not to me...to the lady."

A sneer crossed the big man's face. "To the lady? Vot?"

Coy lowered his voice, but the room was so silent every word was heard.

"I said... you owe... the lady... an apology."

The big man's eyes quickly glanced at the woman and then at Coy. "That ain't no lady. That yust a Klooch. Injan woman."

"Red, yellow, black or white, she's still a lady, and you owe her an apology... Now do it."

"Ha! And you, preacher man, is gonna make me?"

"Don't mistake my meekness for weakness."

Somebody in the crowd said, "Swede, I'd do it if'n I was you."

Swede looked at the Indian girl and then back at Coy. A sneer crossed his face.

"The blazes, I will."

The big Swede suddenly took a swing at Coy. But before he reached half the distance, Coy drew his *Colt* and with the barrel, thumped the big man between his eyes.

The momentum of Swede's fist fell off like a bird shot in mid flight. His knees buckled, and he collapsed into a kneeling position with his back against the counter. Blood trickled down his nose.

A voice in the crowd whispered, "You see how fast he drew that thing?"

Coy ignored the remark.

"Like I said, you owe the lady an apology."

The Swede shook his head a little, evidently trying to focus his wondering eyes. They soon focused on the business end of the drawn *Colt*.

Then, looking at the Indian girl, he said, "Sorry ma'am. My apologies."

The Swede looked at Coy. An ugly sneer crossed Swede's face.

"I'm going to kill you, preacher man."

Coy holstered the *Colt*.

"It is written, 'As righteousness tendeth to life: so he that pursueth evil pursueth it to his own death'."

Looking around the room, Coy continued. "Church services will be at eleven AM, up on the fourth bench, Sunday."

Amidst the hushed whispers and silent stares, Coy made his way to Cap at the other end of the counter. "Now, can you tell me where I can hire some help to get my outfit up there?"

With his elbows on the counter top, Cap leaned forward. He rubbed his chin whiskers with his right hand, evidently trying to hide the grin on his face.

"Well now, some of them *cheechakoes* could probably use the extra cash. But if I was you, I'd go down to the edge of town there, and spread some of that Christian charity amongst the Indians. They need the money more 'en the whites do.

"Ask for John Minook. He's the one that discovered gold here and he owns claim nineteen above discovery, on Little Minook creek.

He has a lot of influence with the Indians. You'll find him at lot six, block eight."

Coy thought a bit. He liked the idea. Perhaps it would open a door of opportunity to witness to the Indians as well. "Excellent idea. Thank you for the suggestion."

As Coy turned to leave, Cap continued. "By the way..."

Coy turned back to Cap.

"That guy you just taught a lesson to, the one they call the Swede? I believe he's one of Bob Duelin's men."

"Who's Bob Duelin?"

Cap glanced around and leaned forward.

"He owns the North Star Saloon. It's a tent, really, with a shingle hanging out front. Anyway, I believe he directs the criminal element we seem to have attracted. He runs a crooked Faro game in the back and fleeces the miners. If anyone complains too loudly, he cheerfully refunds half of their losses, thereby soothing their anger somewhat. A lot of times, when the miner leaves, he coincidentally gets robbed of the money returned to him. No one has been able to prove Duelin had anything to do with it."

"Okay. So why are you telling me this?"

Cap frowned and glanced around again. "Because he makes himself out to be a philanthropist—a do-gooder. He donates money to injured miners and widows and whatnot. Some people like him, some don't. Personally, I don't trust him. Mark my words, when he finds out about you, he'll be workin' an angle."

"Sort of a wolf in sheep's clothing, huh?"

"You could say that."

Coy nodded, and then turned and headed out of the store. On the boardwalk, Coy looked toward the edge of town and headed in that direction.

* * *

Bob Duelin stepped out of the front of the large tent he used for a temporary saloon and emptied a dishpan of water. Just as he tossed the dishwater, he noticed a tall man with a long black coat walking past.

Duelin held the dishpan with one hand as he reached up with the other to remove the cigar from his lips and watched the man walk by.

He blew a cloud of nicotine and wondered what was so familiar about the man. Had he been an acquaintance, one of his past associates, or, more importantly, a victim?

It deserved some thinking on, he decided.

2

C oy Tucker left Minook's cabin and made his way toward the boat landing. He would need some supplies to make it through the night.

On his way there, he passed by a tent with the flaps tied back and a sign hanging out front that read, MISS HATTIE'S HOME COOKING.

The smells wafting out into the muddy street briefly carried his mind back to the days of his youth and his mother's cooking. Coy stopped, closed his eyes, and breathed deeply.

Somewhere in that jumble of home cooking smell, he caught the odor of apple pie.

Coy heard talking as he entered the tent. A long table with a long bench on each side ran down the middle. A red-and-white-checkered tablecloth covered the table. Three men sat at the far end and gave him the once-over. Their conversation ceased. Coy removed his hat and sat at the front to watch the street.

Behind the three men, a large woman who had seen better days came through the back flaps with a tray of steaks and a coffee pot. She set her cumbersome load in front of the men as she eyed Coy.

Wiping her hands on a greasy apron, she made her way to his end of the table.

In a gruff voice, she said, "You can order anything ya want, as long as it's caribou steaks. Rare, medium, or well done. Order all ya want, but ya better eat all ya order. I can't afford to be wastin' food."

Coy tried not to smile. "Well, in that case, ma'am, I'll take one medium caribou steak. And coffee."

"Ain't got no coffee. Only strong, black China tea. I won't have any more coffee 'til the next steamer comes in...and that might not be 'til after breakup."

"Tea it is, then. Um...are you Miss Hattie?"

She quickly looked him up and down. "That's what the sign says."

"Well, Miss Hattie, I thought I caught the heavenly scent of fresh apple pie, and briefly, it and you reminded me of my mother."

Miss Hattie looked him over once again, only more slowly. A slight smile crossed her face.

In a voice that seemed softer, she said, "I'll look around and see what I can find."

With that, she turned and walked away, and the three men renewed their conversation as they ate.

While he waited, Coy recalled the conversation he'd had with Minook. At first, he was disappointed as Minook informed him all the young men were hunting meat for the winter and therefore could not help move his supplies. But after Minook found out Coy was a preacher, he offered his services and agreed to meet him at the landing in the morning.

Coy offered to pay him, but Minook refused, saying, "What I do, I do for Creator...not pay."

Coy was sure he had met a brother in Christ. Coy asked him if he thought they could get it moved in two days.

Minook replied, "Think maybe one day. I have dogs and cart. Dogs pack all same like mans. You... me... dogs... One day."

"I heard it was a .22 bullet, what done 'im in."

The words, even though whispered, sunk into Coy's brain, and brought him back to the present. He dared not look at the three men at the other end of the table. He pretended he was interested in what was happening in the street.

"Yep. The poor chap had powder burns right betwixt the eyes—just like the other uns," another voice said, in a lowered tone. "And the poke he was known to be carrying was gone, too."

"Well, I'll tell ya what," whispered another, "I'd bet ya dollars to doughnuts Bob Duelin's behind all this. Funny how that high-falutin' Southerner has all kinds of money all of a sudden. He's payin' lots of gold for that fancy two-story frame saloon he's buildin'. I heard it from the workers. Where's all that gold comin' from? It ain't from pourin' drinks."

Miss Hattie came through the back tent flap carrying Coy's food. She placed it on the table in front of him, along with a fork.

"Thank you, Miss Hattie. Smells delicious. Would you happen to have a knife to cut the steak with?"

She looked at him as if he had lost his mind. "Use your own. Ain't ya got one? Any self-respectin' man has a knife."

Coy glanced over at the others. They were looking at him and smiling, obviously enjoying the show. *Well, if a show is what they want...*

"As a matter of fact..." he said, as he reached under his coat, "I do have one."

Coy pulled out a bright polished Bowie knife with black buffalo horn scales and a polished brass guard. "Problem is, I shaved with it this morning and it's a might dull."

Coy picked up a twig from the ground and neatly sliced it in two. "Now, if it were sharp, all I would've had to do was hold it up and the twig would have fallen apart from fright."

Miss Hattie's eyes widened. "Now *that's* what I'm talking about."

The other three men laughed. Miss Hattie gave him a wink and walked back to the kitchen.

At the landing, Coy went through his gear for things he'd need for the night. After setting aside his tent, Yukon stove, bedding, ax, a couple of skillets, his sourdough starter, and some other foodstuffs, Coy made up three bundles—one with the tent, the second with the bedding and the food, wrapped in a water-proof canvas tarpaulin, and the third contained the stove and what was left.

Tying the first bundle together with rope, he used the ends to make straps so he could carry it back-pack style. Standing up under the weight of the large canvas tent bundle, Coy grimaced as the ropes deeply sank into his shoulders. After testing the load's balance, he made his way up the hill to his plot of ground.

Three hours later, Coy had packed his three bundles up to the fourth bench to his tent, set up with a fire in the little Yukon stove and his blankets spread out over a foot-thick bed of spruce bows.

He strung the canvas tarpaulin between four trees to catch rainwater. The pitter-patter of rain against the taut canvas tent lent an air of dreariness outside the walls. But inside, bacon sizzled in a cast-iron skillet, while the coffee seethed in the pot and sourdough bread slowly browned on the bottom in another skillet.

Coy was dry, warm, and content. Loneliness was nothing new to him and for the first time in a long time, he felt like he was home.

Coy flipped the sourdough and set the skillet aside. The cast iron would hold heat just long enough to brown the other side until it cooled.

After bowing his head and giving thanks, Coy ate his supper in quiet contemplation, and then crawled under the blankets.

In that state, just between consciousness and sleep, the nightmares returned, and he slipped into a fitful slumber.

* * *

Bob Duelin wiped a shot glass clean with a questionably clean rag, and then placed it on the rough-hewn plank supported by two oak barrels. He filled the glass.

The customer paid his two bits, took his drink, and returned to the Faro game in the back of the tent.

Duelin absentmindedly put the cork back into the bottle and placed the bottle on another plank behind him, as he glanced over the small crowd in the North Star Saloon. The turpentine smell of fresh sawdust on the floor, mingled with cigar and pipe smoke, perfumed the air.

Duelin was no laborer. He preferred other people do the digging. He had learned that providing entertainment was the way to go. A crooked Faro game, gold scales that weighed just a little light, and the surreptitious pinch of a miner's poke was easier than the business end of a shovel.

He was a long way from where he used to be—both mentally and physically. Born in the South, he had fought in the war between the States. From there, he moved West and robbed banks, barely getting away with extraordinarily little cash and a few bullet holes in his coat.

Trying his hand at cattle rustling, he found he wasn't much good at that, either. In 1892, during the Johnson County War in Wyoming, he barely escaped being 'jerked to Jesus' at the end of a rope.

Duelin decided the West was getting too civilized for his taste. Hearing tails of small gold rushes in the territory of Alaska and the Klondike, he and two of his trusted associates decided *that* was the place to be. There was very little law enforcement, and, if one could get in on the ground floor of a major gold strike, one could make quite a killing.

On his way to the Klondike, rumors circulated gold had been discovered on Little Minook Creek and a tent city was hastily being erected at Cap Mayo's trading post.

Duelin correctly surmised the Klondike was filling up fast and there would be too much competition. He had bigger ideas. He wanted to rule the whole mining camp and fleece as many travelers heading to the Klondike and Dawson City as possible.

Rampart, as the tent city had become known, fit the bill. He decided to stay.

So far, things were working out. He had a crew of men framing a fancy whip-sawed lumber two-story building next door that would soon be the new North Star Saloon.

He had five other men on his payroll, as well. Two were confidence men, one was a thief, another was a card sharp who dealt at the Faro table, and the other was an enforcer.

The enforcer was a gunfighter he met on the stern wheeler while coming up the Yukon. If things kept going as well as he thought they would, he could stand to use another enforcer or a confidence man.

What about that new guy? The tall fellow in the long black coat he'd seen walking by earlier. He looked like a man he could use.

There was, however, something mighty familiar about the way the stranger carried himself.

Duelin shook his head, and looked over the gathering evening crowd. Getting the attention of one of his men, he motioned him over with a nod of his head.

Handshaker Bob made his way through the crowd. "What's up, Boss?"

"Where is the Swede?"

Bob snorted and shook his head. "He's nursin' a goose egg on his forehead."

Duelin was puzzled.

"Why? What happened?"

"Oh, he pushed aside a Klootch girl at the trader's store, and one of them *cheechako's* what got off the steamer this morning took exception to it. A big guy in a black coat made him apologize."

"He *made* the Swede apologize?"

"Yep. I had a feelin' about that feller and told the Swede to do as he said. Swede wouldn't listen and cocked back with a fist. Before he could do anything with it, the other guy drew his *Colt* and cold-cocked him between the eyes with the barrel and put the Swede on his knees. 'Twas the fastest draw I ever did see."

A big guy in a black coat? Must be the same cheechako I saw earlier, Duelin thought. *And he is a fast draw.* But Duelin still could not decide why the stranger seemed so familiar.

Oh well, could be a nice addition to my payroll.

"Does this gentleman have a name?"

Bob scrunched up his lips and briefly glanced away as if trying to recall something, looked back at Duelin, and said, "Tucker. I think someone called him Coy Tucker."

Duelin didn't recognize the name, but still, there was something familiar about the man he could not put his finger on.

"Evidently, he's a preacher man. After he made the Swede apologize, he politely invited ever one to church meetin' Sunday."

"A preacher man, huh? Cannot be all *that* tough...but then again, one never knows. I want you to get word to the Colorado Kid. Tell him to meet me here in the morning."

3

The next morning, Coy woke drenched in a cold sweat from his fitful slumber. He knew he'd had one of his nightmares, but it thankfully wouldn't come to mind.

Without moving his head, he scanned the dim interior of his tent while listening for any unnatural noises. All was quiet. The rain had stopped sometime during the night.

Deciding all was well, he reached over and added a couple of dry sticks to the coals in the Yukon stove and opened the draft. Soon, a nice fire crackled away, driving off the morning chill.

While watching the flames, bits and pieces of the nightmare slowly surfaced—a rolling, burning wagon, the ghastly face of a soldier engulfed in flames, stumbling toward a water trough, a volley of gunfire.

The fire in the little Yukon stove popped and crackled, jerking Coy into the present. He shook his head, trying to rid it of those horrible scenes.

After getting dressed, Coy put the skillet he had fried the bacon in the night before on the stove, along with a pot of water to boil. He added more fuel to the fire.

Stepping outside in the dark to relieve himself, he noticed some of the clouds had drifted away, revealing a curtain of weaving, dancing lights on the northern horizon, across the river.

Was that the northern lights he had heard about? He stood in awe and watched the changing colors and patterns of light through the clouds for a good fifteen minutes, or so. Coy was humbled and he bowed his head in silent prayer.

God, thou hast done marvelous things. I have done terrible things. What would people think if they knew my past?

Back inside the tent, Coy set some hot water aside for coffee and washed his hands with what was left. He poured sourdough starter from its container, a hollowed-out section of a birch limb with a birch plug, into a mixing bowl. To that, he stirred in sugar, salt, baking soda, and a handful of wild blueberries he had picked just outside his tent the night before. As the sourdough foamed up, he poured a bit into his sizzling skillet.

While the pancakes browned and the coffee boiled, Coy opened his Bible at random and, with his eyes closed, placed a finger on a page.

Opening his eyes, he read the verse under his finger—*Joshua 1:9.*

Have not I commanded thee? Be strong and of a good courage; be not afraid, neither be thou dismayed: for the LORD thy God is with thee whithersoever thou goest.

Coy closed his Bible and watched the fire burn in the stove as he ate his breakfast.

Later that morning on the bank of the Yukon, Coy separated his supplies into approximately hundred-pound loads. He wondered whether they could get it all moved in a day as Minook seemed to think.

Two wooden boxes contained books. One was filled with songbooks. The other, study books and extra Bibles. The boxes weighed close to a hundred pounds apiece. The rest of the bundles consisted of tools, clothing, food, personal hygiene items, and other sundries.

"You plan on movin' all that by yourself?"

Coy spun toward the voice, ready to draw his weapon.

"Whoa. Easy there. Didn't mean to startle ya."

It was Frank Canton. His hands were held waist high, palms out.

Coy had met Canton on board the steamer *Cleveland* out of Seattle, en route to Alaska.

They found they had both worked for the Regulators during the Johnson County affair—Canton more so than Coy.

With similar backgrounds, the long voyage had allowed the two men to become well acquainted and fast friends. Coy knew if there was anyone faster with a gun than himself, it was Deputy U.S. Marshal Frank Canton.

"Sorry, Frank. Had a guy yesterday threaten to kill me. Thought maybe you was him."

"Yeah, I heard about that. The whole camp's talkin'." Canton lowered his hands and tossed his head toward the bundles.

"Ya need some help movin' your gear?"

"I could do with some help. Minook should be here soon with some dogs and a cart to help pack this stuff up to my place behind the store."

Coy glanced up the path toward the third bench as he spoke. He saw Minook coming down the path to the riverbank. He held on to a rope attached to a cart's back end. The cart was being pulled by three eager Indian dogs.

Coy tossed his head. "Here he comes now."

Canton threw a glance up the path.

"I know him. He told me and my cabin mates about a place on the headwaters of Big Minook where he'd dug some nuggets a few years back. So far as he knows, nobody's been there yet. We figure to head up there in a couple o' days and stake some claims. Wanna throw in with us?"

"Thanks, but no thanks. I got Sunday services to get ready for. Besides, I'd like to get a structure built before the snow flies in a coupla weeks."

Canton smiled and knowingly nodded his head.

"Suit yourself. Just thought I'd ask."

With the cart loaded, Minook shouldered a bundle and headed up to the fourth bench. His dogs pulled the heavy cart behind him. Coy shouldered into his pack. As he hunched his shoulders to adjust the load, he looked at Canton.

"Say, aren't you supposed to be marshaling or something? What are ya doing prospecting?"

Canton's eyes suddenly narrowed as he gazed at Coy. He seemed to stiffen up a bit and his voice took on a different tone.

"Unless something happens that requires more than a miners' meeting, my commission doesn't begin until I reach Circle City. And that's not going to happen until after spring break-up. They have a local constable looking after things 'til I get there."

Canton seems a little touchy about that, Coy decided.

Perhaps from the story going around about the previous deputy marshal. He had been headed to Alaska's interior, so the story goes, and had taken the Canadian route. He got as far as Dawson.

There, in Canadian territory, he stopped and prospected for gold for several months while drawing his deputy wages from the United States. He was soon found out and fired. Canton was hired in his stead.

"Sorry, Frank. I didn't mean to imply anything."

Canton seemed to relax a little. His gaze softened. "No harm done. Let's move this stuff, shall we?"

Later that afternoon, Coy laid his coat and gun belt aside to work on a ground cache to store his grub. It measured six-by-six feet by four feet high and was made of heavy green spruce logs. The strong cache would hopefully stop black bears from robbing his food until he got a proper cache built on stilts, out of their reach.

After marking a length of spruce log for the flat roof, he cut it with a crosscut saw.

"Pardon the interruption, sir."

Coy turned. Two men stood by his tent. He felt adrenalin's sudden hot flush flood his already overtaxed body as he recognized the hawk-nosed face of one man standing a little apart from the other. The other man looked vaguely familiar, too, but Coy couldn't place him.

Coy glanced at his gun belt, ten feet away. No way could he make it. He would be a dead man if he tried. He mentally chastised himself for getting caught too far away from his weapons.

The other man spoke.

"No need for that, friend. I am Bob Duelin. I run the North Star Saloon. I wanted to welcome you to our little mining camp."

Coy wasn't listening much to what Duelin said. He was watching the hawk-nosed man. He saw a slight smile cross the man's face and Coy knew he'd been recognized. He decided to say something first, to maybe throw them off a little.

"Hello, Colorado."

The Colorado Kid dipped his head slightly to Coy. "Boss, this here is Caleb Moore. We used to run together back in the Oklahoma Indian territory."

Duelin glanced from Coy to the Kid, then back to Coy.

"I do not know that name, but... you do look familiar. Were you mixed up in that Johnson County affair, same as me? I nearly got my neck stretched."

Coy's jaws tightened as he suddenly realized who this Bob Duelin fellow was.

"I was. Except I was working on the other side of the law for the Regulators, and you worked a running iron. But that's all behind us, now. As far as I'm concerned Caleb Moore no longer exists. I'm Coy Tucker and I preach the gospel. I've changed."

Colorado snickered.

"Well now, Preacher Coy Tucker, or whatever you call yourself, don't the scriptures say something about the leopard not being able to change his spots? You haven't changed. We're the same, you and me. We were born to it."

"You got it wrong, Colorado. I didn't change myself. I was changed by the grace of God. Nevertheless, like the leopard, I still possess my skills."

Coy watched Colorado's eyes move down and then back up, and he felt naked without his guns.

"Perhaps. You ain't healed right now. Maybe someday we'll find out."

A wave of grief washed over Coy. "For your sake, Colorado, I hope not."

"Gentlemen, please..."

Coy looked at Bob Duelin, who had just spoken.

"...As I was saying, we just came up here to welcome you and give you a little donation to help in your endeavors to bring some religion to our community. Lord knows we need it. Maybe we can help each other out. It is not much but—"

"Mister Duelin, I don't need your money."

"But, surely— "

Coy held up his hand.

"I know your kind. I done told you once. I'm not in that line of work anymore. And if what I hear about you is true, I'll be expectin' you and your men to either come to church regular or move on to greener pastures. Now, if you'll excuse me, I have work to do."

Coy watched as Duelin's eyes narrowed a bit and his jawline muscles bulged.

Duelin glanced over at Colorado and gave his head a slight nod, and then turned and walked away. Coy's eyes met Colorado's for about four seconds before Colorado gave a slight smile, turned, and followed his boss down the slope to the third bench.

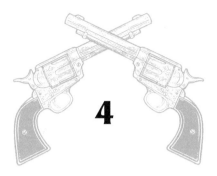

4

Bob Duelin called his usual midweek meeting inside the North Star Saloon with his gang members, just before opening for the evening crowd. He sat down at the Faro table and looked around at the crew seated before him.

A scowl crossed the Swede's face as he reached up and massaged the blue knot on his forehead. Colorado Kid pulled out the makings and began working on a roll-your-own. Handshaker Bob and Camp Robber Freddy sipped their whiskeys in silence.

"Boys, it's Wednesday. Time to call this meeting to order and divvy up."

Duelin looked at Handshaker Bob—an expert at sleight-of-hand games like Three Card Monte.

"How was the take out on the creeks?"

"Pretty good, considerin' things is slowin' down. I think we've seen the last boat 'til breakup. There's termination dust up in the higher hills. Some prospectors are packin' it in an' hunkerin' down for the winter. Those who have sunk shafts are stayin' an' drift minin'. I was able to sell a few fake maps to the gold fields to some of them *cheechakoes* what got off the boat yesterday."

"How is the 'shill' working out? Is he catching on?"

Handshaker Bob glanced at Freddy and then back at Duelin.

"He's doin' great. Still learnin', but, yeah, he's catchin' on."

Duelin looked at Freddy and slowly shook his head as he thought a bit.

"Good. Freddy, you keep learning all you can from your mentor, Bob here and come breakup, when the real rush begins, I will turn you loose on your own. You will have a chance to make even better money. Now, gentlemen..." Duelin said as he looked around at the others. "Time to produce the bounty. Y'all hold anything back and I *will* find out."

Handshaker Bob quickly glanced at Colorado, made eye contact, then looked at the tabletop as he dug into his inside coat pocket.

"It's all here, I swear. All three hundred dollars."

Handshaker Bob produced a poke, placed it on the table, and loosened the drawstrings.

Duelin took the poke and turned it upside down. Cash, coins, and gold nuggets spilled out. Duelin weighed the nuggets, counted the cash and coins, and wrote the amount in a small notebook.

He weighed out ten dollars' worth of nuggets and counted out a hundred and forty in cash and coin. That, he pushed back to Bob.

Bob counted out fifty in cash and coin and gave it to Camp Robber Freddy.

"How about you, Swede? What have you got to show, besides a knot head?"

The Swede blushed as he pulled out three heavy gold pokes and dropped them onto the table.

Duelin reached for them.

"Five hundert in gold, and the Preacher's scalp in a few days."

Duelin hesitated a moment, then picked up the pokes.

"I think not. Preacher Tucker may be of use to me. According to idle gossip, most of the good citizens of Rampart are glad to see him here."

Duelin loosed the strings and poured out the nuggets. That, too, he weighed and wrote the amount in his notebook.

"If the preacher ends up dead, everyone will know you are the guilty party. And, by implication, their anger will fall on me, as well." Duelin looked at Swede and continued. "You know better than to act like anything other than a gentleman in public."

Duelin weighed out three hundred dollars in gold. The rest he put back in the poke and tossed it on the table in front of the Swede.

"I am docking you fifty dollars for acting like an imbecile."

The Swede banged the table with his fist and stood up. Duelin saw the Swede look at Colorado and freeze.

Turning his eyes, Duelin saw Colorado held a *Smith and Wesson* leveled at the Swede's chest. The draw was so quick and smooth, it seemed to Duelin as though the gun had materialized out of thin air. At that moment, Duelin was sure Colorado was worth his wages.

The Swede stammered. "I th... think you're faster than the preacher."

Colorado smiled.

"I think so, too, and maybe someday we'll find out. But for now, the boss says we'll wait. So, we wait. And, if the boss says we act like gentlemen, we act like gentlemen. Savvy?"

The Swede slowly sat down, and Colorado holstered his gun.

Duelin scribbled in his notebook and handed Colorado two hundred dollars. He tucked the notebook into his inside coat pocket. His take of gold and cash, he placed in his poke and set it aside. Duelin looked around the table at the other four men.

"Gentlemen, this meeting has concluded. I want you boys to go back to your cabins or up on the creeks for a few days. Lay low until things cool down a bit. Colorado, you stay here."

Duelin poured a drink for Colorado and himself as the saloon emptied.

Colorado took a sip and set the glass down. "You know, Boss, with the slow down, the boys are wondering how they're going to make pay this winter. Almost everyone in this little camp has been fleeced at least once."

Duelin tightened his jaws a little, took a deep breath, and let it slowly escape. "I have a few projects in the works. The talk is that Dawson is headed for starving times. A lot of miners have already started coming back down the river to other camps or on to Seattle before freeze-up. You may not have noticed, but the population here has increased in the last few days. I am working on a vigilance committee of concerned citizens to help keep the peace. Myself in charge, of course." Looking directly at the Kid, he continued. "I am, by the way, going to require the services of a sheriff."

"Is that it?"

"Is that it? My, my, my. Okay, let me spell it out. Population increase equals more marks for fleecing. Control of the vigilance committee equals less chance of retaliation. That, and with a bigger saloon for them to drown their sorrows and the fact that I got myself appointed coroner the other day, we will make it."

Duelin saw the questioning look in Colorado's eyes.

"Coroner? So...how does that help us."

Duelin took a sip and set his glass down. He felt a smirk cross his face.

"Funny thing is, most people do not want to have to deal with the dead. It reminds them too much of their mortality, I guess. They will gladly let someone else take care of the details."

"I still don't see—"

"It boosts my status in the community. They see me as someone who cares. The more the community likes me, the more tolerant they will be of my boys.

"When these miners die, granted, they do not have much, but they do have rings, watches, and wallets. And when we go through their personal effects to be sent out to nearest of kin—if they can be located—we may find more valuables. A stash of gold or coins maybe. Who knows what happens to that stuff? It will all be forgotten."

"Boss, that ain't gonna to add up to a lot."

"Every little bit counts. Do not forget about the claims. When a miner dies, his claim is considered abandoned. Open for re-staking. Therein lies a golden opportunity, if you will pardon the pun. Each of us could legally re-stake their claims as they become available. With the new wave of *cheechakoes* coming in, those claims can be sold. Or leased."

Colorado suddenly tossed off the last of his whiskey and set the shot glass on the table.

Duelin felt the hackles rise on his neck and he felt like a man spotting a grizzly on the trail at fifty paces. He was instantly alert and keenly aware of every move Colorado made.

"Duelin, I'm tellin' ya, these boys are gonna need more than that. Yeah, a few men will die this winter, most of 'em don't know what they're in for. But we ain't gonna make much on that. As far as the claims go, that has potential, but not 'til next spring. The boys are gonna need something to keep 'em busy this winter or they're gonna get real bored."

Duelin felt the hot flash of anger flood his face. Remembering the dagger under his left arm, he knew at that distance he could draw it and disembowel Colorado in an instant, if need be. But he also knew Colorado could draw and shoot just as fast.

Duelin forced himself to calm down and said, "Look, I am the brains of the outfit. I have got y'all through this far. I will get y'all through the winter. The new building is almost complete and when it is, we shall move in. There will be enough room for three more gaming tables and a stage. We shall make it through the winter—you can count on it. But, if anyone does not like it, he knows which way the river flows. I pay you well, Colorado, for protection and to help keep these men in line and I expect you to do it."

Colorado smiled. "Yes, you do. Now, what are we going to do about Caleb Moore?"

"Who?"

"Caleb, er, Coy Tucker. You know... the preacher man? He as much as gave us an ultimatum. 'Come to church and change your ways or move on to greener pastures'."

Duelin thought a bit. "Yes, well I am not going anywhere. I still think I can turn him."

"I can't believe he's changed all that much. Have you thought about that? Maybe this is a scam on his part. Maybe he's here with the same ideas as you? You know, takin' over this town?"

Duelin had not thought of that. "If that is his game, I now know his true identity, and I am sure he does not want folks to know that. I believe I can use that bit of information to my advantage. If not, we will just run him out of town... or kill him. All in the name of community welfare, of course."

Colorado frowned. "Boss, I ain't got the book learnin' you got, but I have lived some and I'm tellin' ya, it won't be easy. I know what he's capable of when he loses his temper. Or at least, the way he used to be. Below that quiet calm exterior, the cauldron is bubbling."

"How long have you known him?"

"Long enough. I seen the time we had five Buffalo Soldiers transportin' payroll, cornered in a cabin. No amount of firepower we had could drive 'em out. Next thing I know, Caleb is cussin' up a storm. 'I'll fix their bacon,' he says.

"He grabs an empty wagon, loads it with hay, and pulls it to the top of a little rise in front of the cabin. He tied the wagon tongue back and the front axle to the body of the wagon so's it wouldn't veer off course.

"He set that thing ablaze and gives her a shove. Rollin' downhill like that, the wind turned it into a blazing inferno. The impact smashed the door open and scattered fire into, on top of, and along the front of the cabin."

"Bet they came out then."

"Yeah, but it was too late. They kept shootin' at us. Soon, we heard screams inside. I watched in horror as two figures crawled out from under the wagon. Their clothes and hair was on fire. One stood up and stumbled toward the water trough. The other crawled a few more feet, then lay still."

"Did you get the money?"

Colorado looked at Duelin as if he had just seen him for the first time. Then, he shook his head and looked away.

"Nope. The money was destroyed. We walked away with nothing."

Duelin took another sip of his drink. As he set the glass on the table he said, "Sounds like you are afraid of him. Are you getting cold feet?"

Colorado's looked at Duelin, eyes narrowed.

"The day I get cold feet is the day they put me in the ground. When the time comes to get rid of Coy Tucker, I'll consider it my professional responsibility to carry it out. Besides, I have something to prove with him. I think I'm faster than he is."

"Again, that is why I hired you. By the way, there is talk going around about a new confidence man in town. They call him the Blueberry Kid. I think he came down from Fort Yukon or Circle City. I want to talk to him. Now, if you'll excuse me I have some more work to do before I open for business tonight."

Colorado stood and walked out of the tent.

Duelin waited a few moments before he rose, picked up the money and gold, and made his way behind the bar.

There, he knelt and brushed away sawdust and raised a section of the floorboards, revealing a strong box hidden in a hole in the dirt.

Into that, which was almost full of cash and gold dust, he deposited the money and the tally book.

Duelin felt a grin cross his face as he realized he would soon need another strongbox.

5

*C*oy Tucker was still a bit agitated as he cooked his breakfast of bacon and biscuits on his little Yukon stove. He had traveled over two thousand miles to get away from his past, and yesterday it walked back into his life.

He remembered the Colorado Kid as an impetuous, arrogant youngster, fast as a rattlesnake with a gun. It always took a heavy hand to control him, and Coy had his suspicions it was the kid who fired the first shot at the two Buffalo Soldiers back in the Oklahoma territory—the incident that haunted him at night.

And Bob Duelin? Now, there is a sly character. Coy hadn't recognized the name, but he did recognize the face.

He remembered Duelin always seemed to be working an angle. During the Johnson County war, some legitimate homesteaders were falsely accused of cattle rustling by the Wyoming Stock Growers' Association.

Duelin, however, was the cattle thief. Coy didn't know all the particulars, but he recalled Duelin had escaped the noose. It was rumored his jury had been threatened with retaliation by Duelin's gang members if he was found guilty.

Coy decided he wasn't going to worry about Duelin just yet. The Colorado Kid... now, *there* was the danger. Coy knew the Kid was itching to test his mettle in a showdown. Yes, Colorado was fast, probably faster than he had been back when Coy knew him. But Coy had confidence in his own abilities and faith that God would see him through if it was His will.

Coy shook his head and mentally pushed those thoughts aside.

I have to concentrate on the present, he told himself. *Speaking of which, what about the Swede?*

Coy had made him look small in front of everyone in the trader's store. He had seen the hate in Swede's eyes. Coy knew from experience with men like him, the Swede would not let it pass.

But that's not my problem, Coy decided. *I simply righted a wrong done to another human being. If the Swede learned from his mistake and became a better man, then all's well and good. But if not, well... I'll cross that bridge when I come to it.*

Coy knew the criminal element would oppose him, for 'What communion hath light with darkness?' as second Corinthians says. Duelin had already tried bribery and greed.

"And now he knows my real name," Coy whispered to himself. All he wanted to do was spread the gospel and build a structure of some kind to meet in. *Now, it looks as though my past has caught up with me.*

Coy understood most everyone in Rampart knew there was a preacher in town. But there were miners up the creeks who perhaps hadn't heard a minister was available. He felt the need to hike up to the claims and invite them to Sunday services anytime they were in town. If need be, he could hold Sunday services in Rampart, then spend three or four days hiking up through the claims, holding services in some miner's cabin. He could hike back to Rampart in time to rest a day or two before holding services on the next Lord's day.

Coy quickly calculated the day was Thursday. *If I leave now, I can make it at least part way up the trail.*

Word was, however, the trail was in bad shape. He figured he could make it about ten miles or so, inviting all he met along the way. He would spend the night and work his way back to Rampart by Friday evening. That would give him Saturday to get ready for

Sunday services. He didn't know when he'd have time to build a more permanent meeting place. Perhaps he'd have to wait until spring to answer that question.

When breakfast was over, Coy laid out a wool blanket, extra socks, and a change of clothes onto a waterproof tarp. Folding each long edge of the tarp to the middle, he covered the blanket and clothes.

Starting at one end, he rolled the tarp tight so that nothing but the tarp showed, thus creating a bed roll. Securely tying both ends of the bed roll with a single length of rope, he left enough slack between the two ends to be slung over one shoulder and under the opposite arm.

In a haversack, he packed what was left of the sourdough biscuits, a chunk of bacon, a small linen bag containing a handful of dried mixed vegetables, another with ground coffee, a small steel skillet, matches, a small tea pail to boil coffee, and a fishing line with flies.

Realizing he did not have a canteen for water, he made a mental note to stop by Cap's store to buy one.

After strapping on his *Peacemakers*, he pulled on his coat, rain slicker, and hat and then slid a Bible into his inside pocket. With one last glance around the tent, he picked up the bedroll and haversack and then ducked through the tent flap.

A light misty drizzle greeted him.

Coy stepped from the boardwalk through the door of the trader's store and paused to look around. Inside was a bustle of activity.

Miners with less profitable claims were selling or leasing them to the *cheechakoes*. While others, who preferred to stake their own, tried to discover where the good pay dirt was and what ground was left unclaimed. The Swede sold hastily drawn maps of the mining district for twenty dollars a copy.

It seemed to Coy there were more people than there had been when he arrived a couple of days before.

Coy excused himself as he shouldered his way to the counter. Cap Mayo made eye contact with Coy, and a smile crossed his face as he met him at the counter.

"Haven't seen much of ya. Ya settlin' in?"

"Yes sir, I'm trying to. Got a comfortable camp set up and a cache built to keep the bears out of my grub. I'd like to get a log structure up before the snow flies, but I don't know if that's going to happen." Coy glanced around the store. "Looks like the population's swelling a bit."

Cap glanced around the room and smiled.

"Yeah, I'm doing a brisk business. Word is, there's gonna be a famine in Dawson. Too many stampeders and not enough food. The Yukon'll freeze solid in three or four weeks and that'll be the end of the riverboats. It'll be starvin' times in Dawson. Heard tell that some o' them miners are migratin' this way, and from the looks of things, I reckon it's so."

Coy thought a bit as he scanned the shelves behind the counter.

"Think you got enough inventory to hold out?"

"Not at this rate. I'm expectin' one more boat next week before freeze-up, but if it don't make it, I'm going to have to start rationing what I've got left."

"Might be a good idea to start doing that now, just in case."

Coy watched as Cap scanned the crowd again.

"Yeah, you're probably right." Looking back at Coy, Cap asked, "In the meantime, what can I get for ya?"

"A quart canteen. I forgot to bring one with me. I'm headin' up the creeks for a day or two to introduce myself and invite folks to church."

Cap nodded his head, stepped away from the counter, and took a canteen down from the shelf. Walking back, he placed it on the counter.

"That'll be ten bucks."

Coy was mildly surprised as he laid his money down.

"The cost of livin' is a little high, ain't it?"

Cap picked up the money and turned toward the cash register as he said, "Darn tootin', it is."

"I suppose when supplies run low the prices will go up even more."

Cap stopped and looked back at Coy. A scowl crossed his face.

"Mister preacher man, I'm not that kind of trader. The prices will *not* go up. In fact, I will extend credit to anyone who needs it. I've grubstaked many a prospector with nothing to show for it, and probably never will."

Coy looked deep into Cap's gray eyes and knew he was telling the truth. "Captain Al Mayo, you're a good man."

Cap put the money in the cash drawer and turned back to Coy.

"Tell ya what, I've been thinkin' it over some. While you're up there gallivantin' around the creeks, I'll see what I can do about puttin' some of these men to work building us a church building. It'll be a log structure, but we got a saw pit at the edge of town that Duelin's been keepin' pretty busy.

"Maybe we can whip-saw some hardwood birch for flooring and a pulpit and whatnot. Ya know, give it some class. When you get back in a day or two, you can supervise the construction."

Coy was taken aback by his offer. "I...I don't know what to say. I can't afford to pay them."

Cap smiled. "Think of it as community service. It will be voluntary labor. The building will belong to the community, and you'll have use of it long as you're here."

"What about the property?"

"The property will belong to the community as well. I'll give you back your filing fees. It won't cost ya a thing."

Coy thought it over a bit. "You can do all that?"

Cap looked a little indignant. "Why not? I'm the mayor. Tell ya what, I'll get the papers drawn up and you can sign 'em when you get back." Cap stuck out his hand, "Deal?"

Coy hesitated. "Tell ya what, you get the papers drawn up and I'll look 'em over before I shake your hand. I don't want to rush into this."

A slight smile crossed Cap's face. "Fair enough."

Coy turned to head out the door. As he did so, he scanned the room, and there, intently watching him, was the Swede.

6

Coy Tucker stepped onto the board-walk and headed a little north of east, toward the mouth of Minook Creek. The thought of the Swede watching him bothered him somewhat. Evidently the Swede held a grudge.

Aw well, he decided, *I'll be gone for a day or two. That should give him time to cool off.*

Something his mother used to say suddenly crossed his mind. 'He can just get glad in the same pants he got mad in.' He felt a smile cross his face.

At the mouth of the creek, Coy filled his canteen and turned right to follow the slick, muddy trail upstream. The light misty drizzle turned into a steady pattering of larger rain-drops on his hat brim and shoulders.

Coy realized that as wet as everything was, it would be difficult to get a fire going when, and if, he needed one. Stopping at a conve-nient birch tree he looked it over for wisps of curled, paper-thin white bark. He had heard the bark contained oil and would burn even when wet.

Growing up in the Great Plains and the Rocky Mountains, Coy learned early in life what tender to look for to easily start a fire—tender like thistledown, the inner bark of dead cottonwood trees, a bundle of dead dry grass. He always carried some tucked away in a saddle bag just in case he needed it.

The paper of the birch had unfortunately been well harvested by others. Looking around, he found another birch growing a few feet off the trail.

Coy made his way through the wet wild rose and red current brush to the tree and found a few curls of bark along its backside. Another birch standing nearby contained even more. Coy was able to harvest two good handfuls of bark. He placed it inside his haversack.

Making his way back to the trail, Coy continued upstream. In a half mile, the trail pinched out and disappeared between the creek on the left and a steep bluff on the right. It would be a steep slippery climb up the bluff to get through.

Those who had gone before had evidently taken to the creek. Problem was, at that point, the creek ran directly into the bluff and made a ninety-degree turn right, creating a deep pool of water—much too deep to wade.

Coy backtracked twenty yards or so and found a good ford across the creek. Taking out the belt knife he had used to cut the caribou steak, he cut a young stout sapling to use as a wading staff.

Coy waded the swift-running creek and found a well-worn trail through the spongy tundra moss. The trail looked like one long winding mud hole, and in spots, he sunk in almost to the tops of his laced-up boots. Unseen roots and sticks in the mud often tripped him.

He hiked about four miles before he stopped for a break. He was tired and had worked up a sweat. He was used to riding a horse or a stagecoach, not hoofing it himself.

If the whole trail is this bad, he figured, *I won't make it to Little Minook Creek before nightfall.*

He fought his way through the brush back to the creek and rinsed the mud from his boots. The rain steadily fell and the creek, which had been crystal clear, seemed cloudy and deeper.

Looking up the valley, he saw the hilltops were obscured in gray, low-hanging clouds. Coy briefly wondered about his friend Canton and his crew somewhere in those hills. He said a silent prayer for their safety.

Chilled from his sweat, he knew the dampness trapped inside his clothing under the rain slicker could be a killer.

He spotted a stand of spruce growing nearby and noticed one well-branched tree taller than the others. He fought his way through the brush to the trees and ducked under the low-hanging branches of the biggest one.

Underneath, the ground was damp but not saturated like everything else seemed to be. Hacking off some of the dead under-branches with his knife, Coy made a space large enough for himself and his gear.

Some of the larger dead branches easily snapped as the underside wood was still dry. One of them he split with his belt knife using another stick as a baton. Soon he had a nice little pile of dry kindling.

Coy sat down with his back to the spruce and laid out a couple of curls of birch bark in front of him. On that, for insurance, he placed three knots of spruce pitch taken from the tree.

Reaching up, he pulled a small handful of the Old Man's Beard moss which grew on the branches and placed it on the pitch. Over this, in tee-pee fashion, he added the dry split kindling.

His first match took hold and soon a cheerful blaze brought a little warmth and color to Coy's gray and dismal world.

It reminded him of *Matthew 5:16.*

Let your light so shine before men, that

they may see your good works, and glorify your Father which is in heaven.

Coy deeply sighed as he reached out his hands to the warmth.

"Yes, Lord..." Coy said aloud, "that's what I want to do. I want to build a work here for you. But it seems my past has caught up to me, and I'm sure everyone will soon know."

Coy reached over and grabbed his haversack. He pulled out a biscuit and the canteen of water and sat there eating his lunch. The steam from his sweaty clothes slowly rose and mingled with the smoke through the bows of the spruce.

Out in the open, he saw snowflakes mixed with raindrops. He knew the snow would overtake the rain as the temperature dropped. How long it would last was anybody's guess.

He began questioning his decision about coming to the diggings. The trail was more difficult than he had anticipated. His calf muscles had stiffened up after his brief rest. He quickly calculated he had made only a couple of miles from Rampart as the raven flew. By following the winding trail along Big Minook Creek, he had walked about four miles.

Coy took out his pocket watch and looked at the time.

Twelve-thirty. That makes it one mile an hour.

Replacing his watch, he surveyed his surroundings. *Miller Creek should be up that draw to the east,* he figured. *Hunter Creek is at least another three-quarters of a mile further south, and Little Minook probably another mile and a half or more beyond that.*

Coy decided to head back to Rampart. But first, he had to answer nature's call.

Coy rose and ducked under the spruce bows and stepped into the rain and snow. As he stood upright, he saw a fist grow larger as it hurtled toward his face. Coy's reflexes took over and he turned his head to the left just in time to avoid a broken nose. He took the full impact on his cheekbone. A blinding light flashed and bells rang in his head as he staggered back a step.

Coy, in a blind rage, wildly swung—trying to connect with whomever it was. His swing hit nothing but air.

Another jolting punch to the same spot and Coy staggered again. That time his foot caught in a blueberry bush, and he went down in a heap.

"Ain't so tough now are ya, preacher man?"

Coy recognized the Swede's voice and his eyes locked on to his blurry opponent.

Coy tried to stand, but the Swede planted a boot toe in Coy's solar plexus and he lost his wind.

Coy retched as he collapsed back to the tundra.

"I could kill ya right now, preacher man, but the boss said not to. He didn't say nothin' 'bout workin' ya over some."

Coy saw it coming, but there was nothing he could do as another kick landed just behind his left ear.

The loud ringing and dancing lights faded as Coy slipped into unconsciousness.

7

A red-backed vole sat on his haunches and nibbled a blade of grass, as he watched the strange object before him. The odor of blood was familiar and made him hungry, but the tangy odor of sweat was foreign. It could be a source of considerable food through the long winter's night.

The object suddenly stirred. The vole dropped the blade of grass and scampered down a hole to the safety of the dark underworld beneath the arctic tundra. There, it waited. Patiently. Feeling with its feet for movement vibrations and intently listening, it detected no more movement from the upper world.

The vole cautiously worked his way to the outside and peeked out the hole. There, it watched the object again. As the snowflakes grew larger, the object made a sudden noise and moved. Again, the red-backed vole scampered down to the safety of the underworld.

Wet. Coy Tucker felt wet... and chilled.

Is there something wrong with the tent? The fire in the stove must have burned out. But why am I wet?

Something wet and cold softly landed on his eyelid. Coy tried to blink it away, but his right eyelid would not move. Reaching up, he felt it. His cheekbone and eye felt feverish and swollen.

That's strange.

His left eye focused on twigs, and then the leaves of the twigs. They were long, thin, leathery leaves with a fuzzy orange underside.

What was it the old timers called this plant? Hudson's Bay tea, or tundra tea? That was it. But why was he looking at plants?

Another something softly landed on his cheek, and he turned his head to see better with his good eye. A throbbing headache instantly took hold as he watched snowflakes slowly appear out of the lead-gray sky, grow larger, and settle on his face.

His memory swiftly returned. A growl of rage escaped his throat as he sat bolt-upright looking for his enemy. His hand clutches his *Colt* .45. Coy did not remember drawing it. It was there from years of muscle memory and training.

His head swam and nausea welled inside his gut. Coy forced himself to keep it down.

He noticed the sky had grown darker and the rain had stopped, but the snow had taken its place and was steadily falling.

How long had he been unconscious? He could see no evidence the Swede was still around.

The valley was filled with a deafening silence.

Coy eased the hammer down on an empty chamber and replaced the gun in his holster.

Why didn't the Swede take my weapons? Evidently, he was not interested in theft. Only revenge.

Coy rolled over and struggled to his knees. An uncontrollable shiver convulsed through his body. He needed warmth.

Grabbing hold of a nearby alder sapling, he steadied himself as he stood up. He took a step toward his shelter and his head swam. The whole world revolved in a circle. He stumbled and fell to his knees.

Crawling into his shelter, he sat by the fire that had burned down. Taking his hat from the branch stub he had hung it on earlier, he gently fanned the ashes and found what he hoped for—a few coals glowed orange in the dim light.

With shaking, shivering hands, Coy tore small strips of birch bark and, with difficulty, laid them on the coals. A handful of pencil-lead thin dry spruce twigs, protected from the weather under the bows, was added to the smoking bark. A gentle fan of air with his hat brought it to life. He slowly added more and larger fuel.

Holding his trembling hands to the flames for warmth, he watched the fire burn and forced himself to think about what to do next.

The first order of business, he decided, *is to get out of these wet clothes.*

Looking around, he realized there was not much firewood left. He had not expected to stay long.

I just may have to spend the night, now.

Coy added the rest of the firewood to throw more heat, then unrolled his bedroll. Sitting on the tarp, he uncontrollably shivered as he undressed and then wrapped the wool blanket around himself. Sitting cross-legged, he held the front open toward the growing fire to capture as much heat as possible. Within a few minutes, his shakes subsided.

After dressing in his clean, dry clothes, Coy hung the wet ones to dry on limbs surrounding his little shelter. His next order of business was firewood.

He ducked out from underneath the spruce canopy and stood. His head still throbbed, but he was no longer dizzy. His right eye was almost swollen shut as he looked around to make sure he was alone. He noticed the sky had grown even darker as the snow continued to fall.

Close by, he found a couple of dead spruce about as big around as his balled-up fist, and eight-to-ten feet high. Grabbing hold of the nearest one, he pulled it toward himself. It broke at the base with a loud *crack*, indicating it was dry on the inside. The second one was dry, as well.

Those, he dragged to his shelter and shoved them butt-first under the canopy of spruce boughs. He did this several more times until he had a sufficient wood supply to last throughout the night.

Back inside the shelter, he pulled the logs to the fire and arranged the butt ends on the coals. There was enough heat to dry the wood's outer layer, and it soon caught fire.

Coy diced bacon into the kettle and let it fry until the edges were crispy. He added water and a handful of dried vegetables and let it simmer for a while.

When he decided it was cooked enough, he broke up a sourdough biscuit into the mix to thicken it and called it, 'done'. It was a simple meal, but it warmed his belly, and he was content.

Afterward, while sipping his coffee, his thoughts returned to the Swede.

The Swede had caught him totally by surprise. Coy had had no time to prepare.

More than likely, that was how the Swede operated—quickly get the upper hand and fight dirty.

How would the Swede do in a fair fight?

8

To get out of the falling wet snow, Bob Duelin stood under the small portion of nailed-down roof lumber. He watched the carpenters work. It seemed to him they were taking way too long to finish his new saloon's roof.

"Boys! I swear, it will be breakup before you finish this job."

"Sorry Boss, but we're doing the best we can with this thick wet snow."

"It's dangerous up here," someone else replied.

Duelin thought a bit. He knew how to motivate work crews. "Tell you what... You boys finish this roof by dark and drinks are on the house. The sooner we get this structure closed up and a stove put in, the sooner you can work inside where it's warm."

The workers made a rumble of indistinct comments, but Duelin noticed the pace picked up a bit.

He smiled to himself as he looked around the empty room. He envisioned a stage on the south end near where he stood, with a small dressing room behind it.

Looking north toward the main entry and to the right, he could see in his mind's eye the fine mahogany bar he had ordered three months ago. It should be delivered on the first boat after breakup. Corrugated metal for the roof should be in that load as well. Gaming tables and chairs would fill the rest of the space.

A shout from above suddenly jerked Duelin to reality. Quickly looking up, he saw a rough-cut two-by-eight falling through and bouncing off the ceiling joists.

Duelin dove to the side just as it landed on the floor close to where he had been standing.

Duelin scrambled to his feet. Both of his fists were balled up tight.

"WHAT IN TARNATION...?"

"Sorry Boss," one of the carpenters began. "The boards are wet and slick from the snow. I lost my grip."

"Well, you better get a grip or you will be out of a job."

Someone else said, "Sir? It... might be best for you not to stand under us if you want us to work faster."

Duelin knew he was right, and he knew he had been bested. To argue and assert his dominance would make him look even more silly than he already did.

Duelin straightened his coat and brushed as much sawdust from it as he could.

"You are correct, gentlemen. I do not know what I was thinking. My apologies."

He walked out of the building. As he stepped through the rough opening that would soon be the front door, he noticed the Swede limp into the temporary saloon tent next door. Duelin followed him.

Duelin straightened from ducking under the tent flap and saw the Swede standing at the wood stove, rubbing his hands, and working his fingers in the soothing warmth. The Swede's pant legs were soaking wet and mud-stained.

"Looks like you have been on the trail," Duelin said, as he walked behind the rough plank bar.

"Yah."

Duelin picked up a rag and absentmindedly wiped the bar top. "I do not imagine there is much traffic right now."

Duelin noticed the Swede tighten his jaws a bit before answering.

"Not too much. A couple of travelers."

Duelin sensed the Swede did not want to discuss it, but he didn't care. He needed to find out something.

"Heard tell Tucker the preacher man headed up there as well. Did you happen to see him?"

Again, Duelin saw the Swede tighten his jaws before answering.

"Yah. I did."

Duelin wadded the rag into a ball and tossed it on the rough wooden plank. "He had better be alive."

The Swede glanced at Duelin from the corner of his eye. "Was the last time I saw him."

"What is that supposed to mean? I told you to leave him alone."

"You said not to kill him."

"So, what did you do?"

The Swede turned his head toward Duelin, grinned, and held up his fists. "Yust worked him over some."

Duelin felt his heart sink into the midst of his bowels. He slowly lowered his eyes and studied the sawdust on the floor. He looked back at the Swede.

"Swede, I feel you have just brought about the beginning of our tribulation."

9

Coy Tucker woke with a start and noticed, with his one good eye, the sky had lightened up a bit. He slept fitfully through the night, waking every couple of hours to drag the burned butt ends of wood onto the coals. During those times, Coy thought about Bob Duelin, the Colorado Kid, and the Swede.

From what he could recall, Duelin put on airs and fancied himself a southern gentleman from an aristocratic family who would never get his hands dirty. But he was slick as a snake and would steal you blind.

The Kid was fast with a gun, but he was no back shooter. Any trouble with him would be upfront, face to face. Coy knew from his early years the Kid was fast.

Had he gained speed and confidence since then?

And then there was the Swede. He was plain mean. Everyone seemed to be afraid of him and that's what the Swede counted on.

What if someone called his bluff?

Coy was unconcerned with the other gang members. He had seen hundreds of others like them in other mining and cow camps. Men just along for the easy money. Men who drift away at the first sign of trouble like the smoke from his campfire.

But after waking up, those thoughts faded away as hunger pains gnawed at his innards. His thoughts turned to fishing. But first, he needed coffee.

Coy hung his tea kettle over the fire and filled it with water. When it boiled, he added ground coffee, took it off the fire, and set it aside to steep. A couple of minutes later, he gave the kettle a rap on the side and jiggled it. That nicely settled the grounds, and he sipped the coffee straight from the kettle.

Coy watched the gray sky grow brighter as he drank his coffee—the hot liquid chased his chills away. He saw the snow had stopped sometime during the night and all the snow that had fallen had melted. The ground was still too warm to allow snow to accumulate.

By the time he finished his coffee, it was light enough to see well. The sky was overcast, and a dense fog hugged the higher hills.

Digging through his haversack, Coy found his fishing line and flies. He chose one that looked like a mosquito.

As Coy approached the creek, he realized it sounded different. A slight feeling of concern took hold of him. Parting the last stand of willows, Big Minook Creek, now at flood stage, greeted him. He was dismayed the banks were overflown a good fifteen feet on either side of the main channel.

How am I going to get back across this swollen, turbulent stream?

If need be, he could comfortably spend a couple more days waiting for the water to subside, but that would make him late for Sunday services. That would not make a particularly good impression on the town folk.

Coy breathed a silent prayer and then briefly wondered how his friend Canton and his crew were faring further upstream.

After cutting a suitable willow wand, Coy tied one end of the line to the tip and the fly to the other. He found a high bank not too far away that allowed him to get to a back eddy.

Flipping the fly upstream, he watched as it floated and danced on the current, and then lazily swing into the back eddy.

The fly suddenly disappeared in a small ripple, and he felt a tug. Coy set the hook and a fish on the other end fought for its freedom. With a slow, deliberate lifting of the willow wand, Coy was able to lift the dancing creature clear of the water and onto the bank at his feet.

He was amazed at the beauty of the fish flopping before him. It had a large dorsal fin that swept back to a point almost to its tail, peppered with iridescent blue splotches. It was an Arctic Grayling. Coy had heard of the fish, and of their white flesh that smelled faintly of thyme. Coy would eat a fine breakfast.

He had just scraped the leftovers from his skillet onto the tundra in front of his shelter, when he heard voices behind him, a bit up the trail. Coy intently listened and decided three or four miners were making their way downstream.

Coy tossed the skillet into his shelter and worked his way behind the tree, looking for the source of the voices. He presently saw movement in the brush and a glimpse of a red Mackinaw jacket.

As the lead man, who carried an ax, stepped out of the brush, Coy gave a whistle and a wave. The man briefly stopped, waved, and headed toward Coy.

Three others followed, each carrying an ax.

When he got close enough, the man gave Coy a quizzical look and said, "What happened to you? Tangle with a grizz?"

"At the time, it felt like it. Naw, it was the Swede."

"The Swede huh? Lucky to be alive. What'd he take off ya?"

"Just my pride. But as the Good Book says, 'Pride goeth before destruction.' Guess I could do with less pride."

The man in the red Mackinaw looked him over a moment, then said, "Say, ain't you the new preacher what wants to build a church here?"

"That, I am."

The man smiled then and stuck out his hand.

"Pleased to meet ya. I'm Peter Johnson and this here is James Langford, Oliver Miller, and Bill Hunter. We've prospected these parts since ninety-four. Look, if you're headin' upstream, I wouldn't waste my time. Most all the miners are headin' back to Rampart. Most of the diggin's got washed out last night on account of the flash flood from all that rain and snow. We volunteered to go ahead and cut trees to bridge the creek for safe passage."

"Were there any injuries?"

"Couple of men got drowned. We buried one on the bank where we found him. We couldn't find the other one."

Coy was suddenly more concerned about Canton.

"Heard any news of Frank Canton and his crew? They're supposed to be up here somewhere."

Hunter seemed to recognize the name. "Yes sir. Heard tell they was up near the headwaters, in a steep canyon when it hit. Heard tell all but one got out with their lives."

"Don't know who it was?"

"Naw, sir. Couldn't say. Look, you're welcome to tag along with us if you'd like."

It did not take long for Coy to decide.

Turning to the shelter to gather his gear, he noticed a red-backed vole nibbling on the leftover fish.

10

Later that day back in Rampart, Coy staggered into his tent and stashed his wet haversack and bedroll. He was dog-tired as he sat on the edge of his spruce-bough bed and kindled a fire in the stove. He thought about Canton and wondered if he was okay. He knew there was nothing he could do about it, anyway. More than likely, Canton had survived. The man was tougher than nails.

Coy had other things on his mind. He decided he needed to talk to Cap Mayo about holding a miners' meeting, as well as looking over the papers for the building of the new church.

Stepping outside into the misty rain, Coy noticed three or four dead standing trees had been cut and limbed. Another was partially limbed as if work was suddenly stopped.

Coy turned and headed to the trading post. Passersby stopped and stared at him. The swelling on his cheekbone had gone down some and he could see well enough, but the shiner stood out proud as proof of the beating he had received.

Stepping inside, Coy removed his dripping wet hat, shook water from it, and walked up to the counter.

As he replaced his hat, he saw Cap's eyes widen, then a slight grin crossed Cap's face.

"You're a sight for sore eyes."

Coy looked at him for a moment with his one good eye and sarcastically said, "Thanks."

"Sorry. Couldn't help myself. What can I do for ya... One Eye?" Another grin crossed Cap's face.

Coy dead-pan stared at him.

Cap threw up his hands, "Okay, okay. I quit... Seriously, what can I do for ya?"

"Can we talk someplace about a possible miners' meeting?"

Cap nodded his head once. "Sure, follow me."

Coy followed him behind the counter and into a back room. It proved to be Cap's living quarters. His Indian wife, whom he called Margaret, busily made sourdough bread.

Coy removed his hat and sat down at the kitchen table. He briefly explained what had happened.

Cap stared at the table as he slowly scratched his beard. Looking up, he asked, "Did he rob you?"

"No sir."

"Any witnesses?"

"None that I know of."

Cap sighed and looked at the floor, then at the tabletop. Looking at Coy, he finally shook his head. "I'm sorry, but I can't see what a miners' meeting would do. No witnesses—no case. It's your word against his'n."

"Cap, you know as well as I do that Duelin and his gang has got this town buffaloed. The Swede has robbed, beat up, and possibly murdered miners on the trail for a while now. And everybody's too scared to accuse him or Duelin, or any of the others. We, as a community have to start pushing back. I think we can set an example to the community if you have a miners' meeting and back me up. I was wronged and I want satisfaction. Legally."

Leaning forward, Cap squinted his eyes and looked into Coy's. He leaned back and glanced toward Margaret. Coy followed his gaze. Margaret was smiling.

"What say you, my dear?" Cap asked.

"I read once in the Good Book, 'Blessed are the peacemakers'. No peace since Duelin and his boys come. If this bring peace, then it is good."

Cap frowned and looked at the tabletop. He finally shook his head and said, "I don't know. I'll have to think on it."

Silence filled the room, and Cap peered at Coy with his gray eyes. "Somethin' else goin' on?"

Coy gritted his teeth. It was going to be difficult, he knew, but he felt he had to say it.

"My past. I've um... done a lot of things I'm not proud of and—"

Cap Mayo held up his hand. "Hold on! Hold on, young man. You don't need to confess anything to me. Ain't none of us perfect. What's past, is past. You can't change that. One thing you'll learn about Alaska is that it's a land of new beginnings. Most everyone in this land is seeking a fresh start, hoping to strike it rich one way or another. It's like the West all over again. You'll find most people won't give a hoot about what's gone before. What they will judge you on is the here and now—if you got sand in your craw or if you're just whistlin' Dixie."

"Maybe so, but the problem is Duelin and the Kid both know my past. They won't let it rest."

"From what I gather, young man, you have conviction. You believe with all your heart you're doing God's will. And I, for one, believe you are. Like I said before, you ain't like the others, and I will stand with you."

Coy felt as though a great burden had been lifted from his shoulders, but the lump still sat in his throat as he spoke.

"Thanks. You've given me some things to ponder. I just don't know if I'll ever be able to forgive myself for my past."

"Listen, son, I don't know a lot about the Bible, but it seems to me that if the God of all creation can forgive you, then surely you can forgive yourself. Thank and study on that."

"Yes sir, I will. Now about the miners' meeting, take your time. I need a few days to heal up anyway. Now, how about the paperwork for the church building? Do you have them drawn up?"

Cap reached over and picked up a bundle of papers on the table.

"Yes, I do," he said, as he shuffled through the pages. "Yep, here they are."

Cap pulled a couple of papers from the bundle, quickly looked them over, and then laid them in front of Coy.

Coy picked them up and looked them over. They seemed clear enough—straightforward. Coy had not had much time to think about it, however, and something bothered him.

Coy folded the papers in half and stuck them in his inside coat pocket.

"I'll think on it awhile and get back to you. In the meantime, I noticed some dead timber had been cut and limbed on my property. Was that some of your volunteers doin's?"

Cap frowned.

"Yeah, I got a couple of guys up there yesterday after you left to start clearing ground. A few hours later, they were back lookin' awful scared. I asked 'em what was going on. They didn't want to talk much. Finally found out the Colorado Kid had run 'em off. Told 'em, if they knew what was good for 'em, they wouldn't have anything to do with you."

"The Kid, huh?"

"That's what I gathered."

"I guess I'll just have to have a little talk with his boss."

11

Coy Tucker walked into the North Star Saloon tent and quickly glanced around. Duelin stood at the end of the rough plank bar. A bartender was behind the plank wiping glassware. At the Faro table in the back, sat the dealer, Handshaker Bob and Camp Robber Freddy. A man with a black mustache and a black derby hat sat with the Colorado Kid at another table.

Colorado had his back to the wall and toyed with a shot glass on the table with his left hand. His right hung at his side, unseen. All eyes were locked on Coy. The Swede was nowhere in sight.

"Preacher Tucker! Welcome to my humble establishment. We were just getting ready for the evening's business. What can I get you? An ice pack perhaps for that shiner?"

Coy looked at Duelin, who had just spoken. "Some answers."

Duelin slightly smiled. "Well sir, I do not know if I have answers to every question, but I certainly will try."

"I'm sure you have the answers I'm looking for. Did you have the Kid stop work on the church building?"

"The church building? Why sir, we thought they were stealing your timber. We were just trying to protect your interests, is all. You never know what the criminal element is going to do."

"I'm sure you have a pretty good idea."

Duelin looked incredulous. "I am sure I do not know what you mean. I will have you know I am an upstanding businessman in this community. Yes, I keep tabs on the criminal element, but only for self-preservation."

"Meaning, of course, you recruit the criminal element...", Coy nodded his head toward the others. "Like this sorry lot, to work for you and leave you alone. In return, you give them protection."

Duelin smiled. "Something like that."

"Look Duelin, I'm tired and hungry and I don't have time for palaverin'. I'm here to tell ya to keep your men away from my property, unless, of course, they are there to hear God's word and no other reason." Turning his head toward the Kid, he continued, "That goes for you, too, Colorado."

The Kid sat there, smiling. Coy was sure his right hand was on the butt of his cocked pistol.

"Preacher Coy Tucker..."

Coy turned toward Duelin.

"...I am not sure I can do that. However, for a small portion of your Sunday services take, I think I might be able to persuade them."

In a low, even tone, Coy said, "That will never happen."

Duelin sighed, looked at the floor, and said, "That is unfortunate, for we need a good church in this community. It would be a shame if people found out who you really are." Then, looking at Coy, he continued, "Now sir, remove yourself from my premises."

A movement to Coy's right caught his attention. Turning his head, he saw the Colorado Kid standing, facing him, thumbs tucked in his gun belt.

Coy looked back at Duelin.

"Don't mistake my meekness for weakness."

Back at the church tent, Coy wearily plopped on his spruce bow bed, still dog-tired and hungry. It had been a long day, and he had not eaten anything but the grayling and sourdough biscuit for breakfast that morning. He knew if he sat there long enough, his muscles would stiffen and he would not want to do anything but sleep.

Forcing himself to move, he got a fire going in the stove and put a wash pan of water on to heat. After washing up, he held the wash rag, soaked in the hot water, to his cheekbone and the back of his head. He didn't know if it would help, but it sure felt good.

After giving thanks for the Lord's provision and asking for guidance in his life, he made a pot of strong black coffee and opened a tin of potted ham and another of peaches.

As he ate, he thought of the day's events. In his youth, he would've already taken revenge. He would've tracked the Swede down and killed him. And if the Colorado Kid got involved, then him as well, or, if the Kid got lucky, Coy'd be dead. Either way, it would be over. Coy was thankful he wasn't that type of person anymore.

But then again, it would sure eliminate some headaches...

Lying down in his blankets, he closed his eyes, opened his Bible, and pointed to a page. Opening his eyes, he read the words under his finger. Second *Corinthians 5:20.*

Now then we are ambassadors for Christ, as though God did beseech you by us: we pray you in Christ's stead, be ye reconciled to God.

Ambassadors, he thought to himself. *A representative of one country, or entity to another. A representative of one country cannot run the affairs of another. If I am an ambassador of Christ, as in, a representative, then I, in good conscience, should not be in partnership with the local government. There's just too much room for misunderstandings and abuse of power.*

A verse suddenly surfaced in his brain. *"No servant can serve two masters."*

Coy knew then what bothered him about the church paperwork.

12

Saturday morning downed and Coy Tucker awoke feeling completely rested. He realized he could not recall his dreams. He had not had any nightmares. That happened sometimes.

Throwing back his tent flap, he noticed the continual drizzle of rain over the past four days had stopped and the sun peeked through the clouds.

After breakfast, Coy put on a pot of beans to simmer throughout the day for that night's supper. He had hoped to spend a quiet and peaceful day, studying and getting work done on the church building. His mind, however, mulled over Cap's offer about the community donating labor and property to the church project. He felt grateful for the offer, but it did not sit well with him. He hoped Cap would see it from his perspective and understand.

Coy walked into the trader's store and glanced around. It was almost empty. Another man and a woman were the only people present. Stepping up to the counter, he scanned the shelves for anything he might need.

"That shiner's lookin' a lot better. How's the back of your head where he kicked ya?" Cap asked in a low voice as he approached Coy.

Coy looked at him and said, "Good. It's still sore of course, but I've had a lot worse."

A slightly uncomfortable silence fell between them as Coy tried to decide how to open the conversation. Cap spared him the decision.

"So, have ya had time to think it over? About the paperwork for the church, I mean."

Coy slowly exhaled. "Yes, I have. I'm going to have to decline your kind offer, I—"

"What?" Cap looked somewhat hurt and perplexed.

"I'm sorry. It's nothing against you. In fact, I thank you for the offer."

"Well, then what in jumpin' Jehoshaphat's the problem?"

"I guess you could say it goes back to our founding fathers. Separation of church and state. I'm not saying you or the community *would* mind you, but if I was to enter into a contract with the community, they would have a say in what the Lord leads me to do and how I do it. As the good book says, we cannot serve two masters."

Cap blinked a couple of times, then said, "They'd never do that."

"Maybe not. But to avoid any misunderstandings, I think it's the right thing to do. This is something I feel led to do, and I must do it. Now, if individuals on their own wish to lend a hand, then that's a different matter."

Cap looked around the room a couple of times, sucked his teeth, then looked at Coy.

"I get your drift. I can see where that might be a concern. If I was in that position with the store and somebody wanted me to run it like they wanted it run, that just wouldn't float my boat. No siree."

Coy stuck out his hand. "Still friends?"

Cap looked at Coy's hand then at Coy's face and smiled as he took the offered hand.

"Yes sir. Still friends. And if I've said it once, I've said—"

"I know. I know. I'm not like the others."

Later that afternoon, the sun shone warm in the partly cloudy sky. Coy took off his shirt. Almost all the snow had melted.

He had just finished limbing another log with the single-bit ax. That made five logs on the ground—seven, counting the two which had already been downed by Cap Mayo's workers.

A good start for the church building.

Setting down the ax, he stretched his back muscles and moved his shoulders in a circle, working the weariness out—the kind of weariness that makes a working man feel alive.

Picking up the ax, he turned and sunk the keen edge into a stump to protect the edge of the ax, as well as himself should he happen to fall.

One can never be too careful.

As he turned back, he noticed a woman on the other side of the tent walking up the bench toward him. Being a cautious man, Coy quickly glanced at his gun belt lying next to his shirt and moved toward it while glancing around and intently listening.

Deciding all was clear, he slipped his shirt on and buttoned it up, and then wiped the sweat from his face and neck with his bandanna.

The woman looked hesitant and uncertain.

"Wonder what she wants," he said, half out loud to himself.

Coy gathered up his gun belt and started to put it on.

On second thought... He picked up his coat and laid it over his forearm to cover up the rig in his hand.

Walking around the tent, he stepped out in front and gave her a slight wave. She seemed somewhat relieved, and yet, somewhat distraught as she stopped thirty or so feet away.

"Are you Reverend Tucker?"

Reverend? No one's ever called me that before, Coy thought.

Thinking to lighten her mood somewhat he said, "Ma'am, I've been called a lot of things in my day, but that's a first. You can call me Preacher or Paster Tucker, or just plain old Tucker. Just don't call me late for dinner."

Coy saw a quick smile flash across her face. "What can I do for you, Miss..."

"Woolbright. Mrs. Woolbright."

Coy noticed her eyes were red as if she had been crying.

"My husband," she continued, "is on his way to the North Star Saloon, if he isn't there by now, and I'm afraid he's going to get himself killed."

Coy took a couple of steps toward her. "Why? What's wrong?"

Mrs. Woolbright sobbed. "Oh, please help me. There's no tellin' what he will do."

"Okay, okay. Come with me and tell me as we go. What happened?"

Coy handed her his coat as they walked toward the saloon.

"He met a fella, said he had an inside scoop on a claim for sale that could produce real good and wanted to know if Clyde, my husband, wanted to go in fifty-fifty. He agreed to."

This ain't going to turn out good, Coy thought as he tucked his shirt in.

"Anyway, this fella put five hundred dollars in an envelope and my husband put in our five hundred. That's all we had left to get by this winter."

Coy buckled on his gun belt as they passed the trader's store.

"The fella," she continued, "stuck it in his coat pocket, but then took it back out and said to my husband, 'On second thought, you take this money to the claim owners. But you have to do it now before somebody beats us to it. It's number thirteen above discovery on Miller Creek. I've got to take care of some business and I'll be right up.'"

Mrs. Woolbright handed Coy his long black coat.

"Let me guess. Your husband found out later the envelope he received was filled with old newspaper clippings. And this 'fella' never showed up." Coy pushed his arms through the sleeves of his coat.

Mrs. Woolbright sobbed again. "Not only that, but the claim owners had no idea what my husband was talking about. The claim wasn't for sale. He just got back from up there what with all that rain and flooding they had. He nearly drowned trying to get back."

By now they stood in front of the North Star Saloon.

Coy turned to Mrs. Woolbright. "What does this 'fella' look like?"

"Bl... black derby hat, thick black mustache, black bow tie, and vest. They call him the Blueberry Kid."

"I've seen him before. And your husband? Hurry ma'am, we may not have much time."

"Blue checkered Mackinaw jacket. His favorite color."

"Good enough. Now stay out here. It may get ugly fast."

Coy stepped through the saloon tent flap and identified a man in a blue Mackinaw standing at the bar and staring hard at the back of a man in a black derby hat who sat at a card game in the back.

Just as Coy spotted Mr. Woolbright, Woolbright downed the last of his beer, banged the mug on the bar, wiped his mouth with the back of his left hand, and pulled a pistol out of his waistband with his right.

Woolbright started toward the card game.

Coy grabbed him by the shoulder, spun him around, took his gun, and shoved him into the waiting arms of his wife outside the tent.

"Keep him out here!"

Stepping back into the saloon tent, Coy shoved Woolbright's gun into his waistband and glanced around the interior.

He saw Duelin standing to the right. His lips were curled, and he looked as though he was about to say something. Coy pointed his finger at him and glared into Duelin's eyes. Duelin evidently thought better of it because he closed his mouth and took a step back. Colorado was nowhere in sight.

One of the patrons passed by Coy heading for the exit. Coy made eye contact with him. "What's wrong?"

"That fancy fella's cheatin' but I can't prove it. There's gonna be trouble."

Coy turned his attention to the card game and walked up behind the Blueberry Kid, who had just drawn a card. Coy looked at Blueberry's hand over his shoulder. Full house.

Coy poked his .45 in Blueberry's ribs and said, "Nice pile of cash there."

Coy saw Blueberry stiffen.

"Do I know you?"

"Probably not, but that doesn't matter."

The other players got up to leave and Coy

shook his head. "No, no, no, gentlemen. Stay. This won't take long. Hand me the discards."

One of the players raked them together and handed them to Coy. While holding them in his hand, he fanned them out with his fingers and studied the edges.

Tossing them back on the table, he said, "Those cards are marked. Study the design on the backs. You'll find they're not all the same. Got any extra cards, Mr. Blueberry?"

"Are you accusing me of cheating, sir?"

"I'm not accusing you of anything. I just asked a simple question. Now, keep your hands on the table easy like, and don't move."

Coy reached into Blueberry's left sleeve with two fingers and removed an ace of diamonds. One of the players cursed.

"So now what, stranger?"

"You owe Mr. Woolbright five hundred dollars. Something about a bogus mining deal."

"Mr. Woolbright? Look, that was all a joke. I was going to pay him back. I was doing him a favor. I was teaching that *cheechako* a lesson about trust."

Blueberry's left hand slightly moved to the edge of the table. Coy jabbed Blueberry's ribs, reminding him of the .45.

"Trust huh? I don't trust you. Move that hand back any farther and your days of dealin' are done. Now... move that hand nice and easy back to the money and count out five hundred dollars. No more, no less. You know, you should thank me. I just saved your life. Two seconds later, and Woolbright would have killed you."

The Blueberry Kid counted out exactly five hundred dollars and, with his right hand, handed it over his right shoulder. Coy took the money and stuffed it in his inside coat pocket.

"Thank you, gentlemen, for your indulgence. Sorry to have disturbed your game. You gentlemen can divvy up what's left. Have a good day."

And then on second thought, he added, "By the way gentlemen, church services are tomorrow at eleven o'clock. Hope to see you there."

Coy took a step back and quickly scanned the saloon's interior before making his way out. Most everyone sat or stood stock still with their hands in plain sight. Then, a chill suddenly ran up his spine as he recognized Colorado standing by the tent flap.

But Colorado didn't move. His hands were held up, chest high.

"It's okay preacher, I've got your back. Or should I say I got Colorado's back?" Canton peered around the back of the Colorado Kid and smiled.

"Canton! I was worried about you. Made it, I see."

Coy noticed Colorado's expression change from grim determination to possibly fear.

"Yeah, it was a heck of an expedition. Remind me to tell ya about it later."

Colorado broke into the conversation as Coy worked his way up to Colorado and the doorway. "Canton? Frank Canton?"

Coy stopped and met his gaze. "The one and only."

The corner of Colorado's lip went up in kind of a sneer. "You are one lucky hombre. I would have had you if it weren't for your friend here."

"Luck? I'll tell ya something I learned a long time ago, Colorado. Luck is what a fool calls it when God gives him a break."

13

"Pull up a stump and have a seat," Coy said, as they entered his tent.

Canton followed him. "Don't mind if I do. Got any coffee on?"

Coy picked up the coffee pot and sloshed it around. "There's a little left from this morning. Probably be best to make a fresh pot. There're beans on the stove I've been cooking all day. Probably ready if you want some, and welcome to 'em."

Canton smiled. "Never been known to pass up a good meal."

Coy took a step toward the tent flap, then stopped and said, "By the way, thanks for watching my back down there."

"Aw, no problem. I'd just got back to town and was headin' to the trader's store when I saw you go into the saloon. Then I saw that other feller, Colorado I think you called him, slip in behind you. I thought, 'this don't look good'. So, I stopped and asked the lady out front. She gave me the low-down. I figured I'd step in just in case."

"Well, glad you did. Mrs. Woolbright sure was thankful when I handed her the money. Think her husband learned his lesson?"

Canton smiled. "Well, if he didn't, I'm sure he's learning it, now."

Coy went outside, dumped the old coffee grounds, then dipped water from the rainwater tarp. Back inside, he placed the pot of water on his little stove and stoked the fire.

"I was concerned about you when I heard about the flash flood up on the headwaters. Where I was, the valley is wider, so the water level rose about four feet, is all." Coy said as he shut the stove door.

Canton looked a little surprised. "You were up on the creeks?"

"Yeah, got about as far as Miller Creek but decided to head back. Then things got a little ugly and I ended up spending the night under a tree."

"That black eye got anything to do with it?"

Coy took the lid off the bean pot. "Yeah. But enough about me." He stirred the pot of beans. "Evidently you boys got out okay," he said as he added water to the beans.

"Huh. Just barely. We was in a steep canyon when we heard the water roarin' down on us.

We couldn't climb up, so we had to hightail it downstream ahead of the flood."

The coffee water churned then bubbled. Coy removed it from the stove then added a quarter cup of grounds. He put the lid on to steep.

"Earlier," Canton continued, "two of our party had got turned 'round and went up the wrong draw. On our way out, we found one of them, but the other had died of exposure. He wasn't dressed right for this weather. Of course, none of us were properly outfitted. We were in too danged of a hurry to be the first to get up there. I sure learned my lesson about being prepared in this country."

Coy picked up the coffee pot, gave it a little shake to settle the grounds, and then poured a cup and handed it to Canton.

Canton took the cup. "Thanks. And that tundra," he continued, "hikin' through that stuff is like...is like walkin' on a two-foot-thick lumpy mattress all day long. It will flat wear you out."

Coy got a tin plate and filled it with beans and handed it and a spoon, to Canton. Canton set his cup down and accepted the offering. "Thanks. Now, what about your story?"

Between mouthfuls of beans and bis-cuits washed down with coffee, Coy related his story.

Canton took a sip of coffee, looked at Coy for about four seconds, and then said, "So, what are you going to do about it?"

"Well, deep down I know this affects more than just me. It affects the community. Problem is, everybody here is too scared to deal with Duelin and his boys. I'm looking into calling a miners' meeting. Set an example to the community. Show 'em they need to stand up to the criminal element."

Canton took another sip and quickly glanced Coy up and down as he swallowed. "What if they find him innocent?"

"Well, if they do, they do. I'll cross that creek when I come to it. At least it will send a message. Maybe others will find the guts to stand up to Duelin and his gang."

Canton took another sip of coffee, swallowed, then inspected the contents of his cup for a minute. Then, looking up he said, "I gotta ask, bein' a lawman and all, ya got any witnesses?"

"No, I don't. It was just him and me out there in the rain and snow."

Canton drained the last of his coffee and held out his cup for more. "Ya know, it's gonna be mighty hard to get a verdict. It's your word against his. And knowin' Duelin's kind, he will probably try to pay off the jury or threaten them for a favorable vote."

Coy refilled Canton's cup and his own. "I hadn't really thought of that."

Canton took a swig of coffee. "Say, didn't you mention you were up by Miller Creek?"

"Yeah. Pretty close."

"Well, wasn't that Woolbright fella up there also, about that time?"

Coy thought a bit. "Mrs. Woolbright did mention Miller Creek as her husband's destination. He could have been up there about that time or just after."

Canton smiled. "Let me do some investigatin' and see what I can dig up for ya."

14

Sunday morning dawned clear and cool. Coy Tucker rose early after a fitful sleep and cooked his breakfast.

Later, while lingering over his last cup of coffee of the morning, Coy wondered if anybody would show up. And if they did, he hoped to make a good impression. He was also concerned because he had an idea of what to preach about, but no concrete thoughts.

Exodus 4:13 sprung to mind. *Now therefore go, and I will be with thy mouth, and teach thee what thou shalt say.*

Coy rearranged his spruce-bough bed to the back of the tent, along with his gear. He hung a canvas tarpaulin curtain between his gear and the rest of the floor space, separating his living space from the makeshift auditorium.

He opened the box with songbooks and the other of Bibles and set them by the open tent flap for attendees to use during the service.

Looking around, Coy decided all was ready. There were no seats. Those in attendance would have to sit on the ground or stand.

After washing up, he changed into his Sunday go-to-meeting clothes, strapped on his twin *Peacemakers*, and shrugged into his dress coat.

Coy patiently waited and then checked his pocket watch. It read ten forty-five.

Will anybody show up for the first service?

Hearing voices, he stepped outside and looked down the path. A group of people, led by Captain Al Mayo, along with his wife and children made their way toward his tent.

A little further back, he saw John Minook and his family. One of the group members, a large, broad-shouldered man carried a guitar. Coy was pleased to see they would have a musical instrument to accompany the singing.

Coy greeted each person as they entered the tent while looking over the crowd for Duelin or any of his gang. It wouldn't surprise Coy if Duelin used this opportunity to cause trouble.

"Good morning... Make yourselves at home... Good morning... Glad to see you brought a guitar. Would you accompany our song service?" he asked the broad-shouldered man.

"Yes sir. Be glad to."

The tent was filled with visitors and both tent flaps were tied back to completely open the front so others standing outside could hear and participate in the services.

He hadn't seen any sign of Duelin, so Coy made his way to the front of the congregation with his songbook.

"Good morning. It does my heart good to see you all here this morning. My name is Coy Tucker, and I am a Baptist preacher of the gospel of Christ."

They sang a hymn, accompanied by the guitarist, and then Coy began his sermon.

"Follow along in Ecclesiastes chapter three, starting with the first verse. *'To everything, there is a season, and a time to every purpose under the heaven: a time to be born and a time to die; a time to plant, and a time to pluck up that which is planted; a time to kill...'*"

"Excuse me, ladies and gentlemen."

Everyone turned to see who had spoken.

Duelin, along with the Colorado Kid pushed their way into the tent. Duelin grasped his lapel with his left hand and continued speaking.

"Pardon this most inopportune time, but in the interest of civility, I must give voice to my concern for this community's welfare." Duelin pointed the finger of his right hand at Coy and continued, "It seems we have an imposter here, in the guise of this so-called preacher."

A low murmur ran through the congregation. Coy felt anger rise in his chest, and he clenched his jaws as he felt heat flush his face. Should he draw and back Duelin and the Kid down?

No, he decided. *Let him make the first move.*

"Mr. Duelin, if you're here to..."

"Now most of you know me," Duelin continued, as he lowered his hand, "I'm an upstanding proprietor in our fair community, and lacking proper law enforcement, I try to keep tabs on the criminal element." Duelin raised his hand and pointed at Coy as he continued to speak. "I have it, on good authority, that his man's real name is Caleb Moore—a man with a history of lawlessness throughout the West."

A collective gasp erupted as the congregation looked back at Coy.

"Ladies and Gentlemen..." Duelin continued, as he replaced his hand on his lapel, "I thought it my responsibility, as a concerned citizen, to let y'all know about this man. I, along with other proprietors of our fair community, propose to put a stop to the lawless acts of many *cheechakoes*.

"We hereby summon all good citizens to a meeting at the North Star Saloon at noon today, at which time these matters will be discussed. Let this be a warning to all new-comers disgracing our fair city."

Duelin locked eyes with Coy, gave a little smile, then turned to leave. Some in the congregation followed.

Coy stepped forward and stopped, feet shoulder width apart.

"Just a minute there, Duelin. Wanna tell *your* story?"

Duelin stopped and turned toward Coy. The Kid quickly glanced from Coy to his boss and then back at Coy. His eyes narrowed as he slowly moved his coat flap behind his holstered *Smith and Wesson*.

Cap cleared his throat and said, "Now, wait a minute everbody. I have something to say as well. You gonna take the word of one man?"

The tension in the air eased a bit. A low murmur began in the congregation.

"Yeah! What about it, Preacher?" someone asked.

"What's your story?" asked another.

Coy Tucker raised his hand for silence. He felt a lump rise in his throat again as the murmuring died down.

"Without bringing up details, I confess that, yes, I was a hounder in my younger days. I was raised in church. I heard the things

God had said, but I rejected it. I turned to rustlin' cattle, robbin' people, and holdin' up stagecoaches and banks. And because of that, I learned to shoot fast and straight. Yes, I have killed men, but always in self-defense. Never murder."

Coy's eyes locked onto Duelin. "What about you? Can you say you've never committed murder? Wanna tell 'em about *your* past?"

Duelin glared at Coy for about six seconds, then turned and left the tent.

The Colorado Kid stayed.

Coy looked at each person left standing in the tent.

"I loathed the man I had become and even though I knew I didn't deserve it, I asked God for forgiveness and salvation. I asked him to take over my life and lead me in the paths he would have me follow. Though I'm still haunted by the memory of scornful and repulsed faces of men and women I've wronged," making eye contact with Colorado, he continued, "I am no longer the man I used to be. I vowed then and there to fight evil wherever it may take me." Coy looked over the crowd and said, "So, there you have it, a sinner saved by the grace of God."

Silence filled the room. Colorado left the tent.

Cap stepped forward and stood by Coy.

"How many of us are perfect? How many of us have never done anything wrong?"

Someone in the back asked, "Don't the Bible say somethin' about *'let he who is without sin, cast the first stone?'* I say let's give him a chance. See if he's true to his word."

Another murmur ran through the crowd. Several more people left the tent. Looking around, Coy saw that Cap and his family, Minook, his wife and kids, the guitar player, and three or four others were the only ones who remained.

The guitar player spoke up. "I reckon you should get on with your services, Preacher. We ain't got all day."

Later that afternoon, Coy took a break from his labor. He had notched and laid two courses of logs for what was to become the Rampart Baptist Church. Looking at his blistered palms, he smiled. Cap Mayo had once told him his hands were soft, that he hadn't lately done much work. That was true, he hadn't. It felt good to again be industrious—to create something.

Coy stretched his arm and back muscles. They were sore and achy from lifting logs and chopping notches—fitting them together as if they grew that way. It was a good kind of soreness. The kind that comes from an honest day's work.

But what if this is all in vain?

His past had caught up to him at last. Duelin had successfully driven most of the congregation away that morning.

Will anyone come back? Who knows?

He decided the only thing to do was to keep pushing ahead—build the building and preach His word.

Coy grabbed his canteen, pulled the cork, and downed the last swallow. He pulled a clean bandana from his hip pocket and ripped a couple of bandages from it for his hands.

He was finishing that task when he heard a voice.

"Hello, the camp."

Looking up, he recognized the guitar player walking toward him. "Come on up."

As the guitar player came closer, Coy tightly wrapped the palm of his right hand. He tucked the loose end under the wrapping on the back of his hand and then made a fist to test it.

"Blisters?" the guitar player asked as he approached.

Coy studied the large, broad-shouldered young man standing before him. He had a longish face with blue eyes, thick jowls, and a large chin. The corners of his mouth turned downward in a permanent frown. He didn't look like he was packing a gun, but then, you never know.

"Yeah, I haven't done this much physical labor lately. Gotta toughen my hands up some."

"Got any alum?"

"No."

"The tradin' post has some. Make a warm brine out of it. Then add some salt to it and soak your hands in it at night, and then wrap 'em up like ya just did. It will dry up the blisters and help toughen your hands."

"You a doctor?"

"No sir. Watched some bare-knuckle boxers do it. Did it myself and it worked."

"Thanks. I'll keep that in mind. What do they call you in these parts?"

A flicker of a smile appeared at the corner of the young man's mouth. "Rex Beach."

"So...what can I do for ya, Beach?"

"Well, sir..." Beach swallowed, glanced at his feet, and then back at Coy, "...I saw ya workin' on the church, and I admire the way you stood up to Duelin, and I wondered if ya, you know, needed any help. With the logs, that is."

Coy thought a bit. *This is unexpected.*

"My past doesn't bother you?"

"We've all got a past. I once studied to be a lawyer. I hope you don't hold that against me."

Coy couldn't contain a chuckle. "That *is* a pretty low-down occupation, all right." Coy nodded to a stand of dead spruce. "Knock yourself out."

* * *

Bob Duelin stepped out of the North Star Saloon tent and headed for the outhouse in the back. He was still feeling smug about breaking up Coy's little church service that morning.

Who did he think he was, coming into this community and openly confronting his men for perceived wrongs? Walking in free as you please and making one of his men pay back the money he stole fair and square?

Duelin figured he had a pretty good grip on that little mining camp, but ever since that preacher man got there, he had felt his grip slip a bit.

Reaching the back of the saloon, Duelin had taken a few steps toward the outhouse when he glanced up the hill toward Coy's tent.

Duelin stopped in his tracks and removed the cigar clenched between his teeth.

About four rounds of logs had been cut, peeled, and notched into place on the church building.

There is no way Coy could have laid all those logs himself, he thought. *Somebody is helping him.*

Duelin spit, replaced the cigar between his teeth, and trudged to the outhouse.

Back inside the North Star Saloon, Duelin sat down at a table with Colorado.

Duelin heavily sighed and said, "The preacher has got four courses of logs laid in place for the new church building, just since noon when we were there. Somebody must be helping him."

Colorado toyed with his empty shot glass. "He is a persistent cuss."

"You would think, after that slap in the face I gave him this morning, he would think twice about his persistence."

"Boss, I know from experience, he won't be pushed around."

"Yes? Well, the Swede beat the snot out of him, and he did not do anything about it. I just exposed his past to the congregation, and most of them walked out. And yet, he is up there still building on that church of his. He just turns the other cheek."

Colorado looked up from his shot glass at Duelin. "The problem is Boss, he's gonna run out of cheeks."

15

Monday morning dawned cloudy and cool. Coy broke the skiff of ice on his rainwater catch basin and dipped water out for coffee.

Back inside the tent, he set the coffee pot on the stove, along with an empty skillet.

"You were saying you have some good news?"

Canton glanced up at Coy and nodded his head. "Yeah, mostly good. It took some doin' but he finally remembered seein' the Swede headin' up Minook Creek. The timin' works out with your story."

"Well, that's good," Coy said as he mixed flour, salt, sugar, and baking soda in with some of the sourdough starter. "Why did it take 'some doin'?"

Canton smiled. "Didn't want to answer my questions. Embarrassed about being swindled, I guess."

Coy turned the dough out into the warmed skillet—well-seasoned with bacon grease. He covered the bottom of the skillet with the dough, and set it aside to raise. "So, how did you convince him otherwise?"

"I reminded him that you had saved his life *and* probably his marriage. That, and the look his wife shot him when I said that, convinced him otherwise."

"Yeah, never underestimate the power of 'the look' from a woman scorned."

"That in the Bible somewhere?"

Coy placed another skillet on the stove top to heat up. "Not that I'm aware of. Nevertheless, it's true."

"That eye looks a lot better. Still hurtin' any?"

Coy glanced at Canton and wiped his hands on a clean rag, and then settled back against his duffel. "Nope. Feels pretty good."

Silence filled the tent as conversation died and the patter of rain on the canvas tent replaced it. That, and the crackling fire and pleasant warmth it radiated lulled each into their own thoughts.

With an angry hiss, the coffee water suddenly boiled over. Coy handed Canton the coffee grounds as Canton lifted the coffee pot off the stove. "Put some grounds in there while I put the sourdough on."

"Looks like the church building is coming along. You have any help?" Canton asked as he spooned grounds into the seething water.

Coy placed the smoking hot skillet from the stove top, upside down over the skillet containing the sourdough.

"Yeah. A fellow who calls himself Rex Beach came up after morning services yesterday and gave me a hand with a couple rounds of logs. He's right handy with an ax."

Canton replaced the lid on the coffee can, and put the lid on the pot. He set it aside to keep it from boiling up. "I got some time on my hands. I'll help ya today. If this Beach feller comes back, we can probably get you up to eave height."

"That would be nice. I can use all the help I can get." Coy's thoughts trailed off as he reran their conversation through his brain.

"Something botherin' ya?" Canton asked.

Coy glanced at Canton, who held out a cup of coffee for him. "Sorry. You said it was 'mostly good' information. So... What's the bad?" He accepted the offered cup.

"Oh, yeah, that. Well... Seems as though Woolbright don't want to testify. He was pretty adamant about it. I figured to give him last night and this morning to think it over, and to let his wife work on him. If that don't do the trick, then I'll work on him. He'll come around."

"Hope so. Everything kinda rests on him."

Later that evening, Coy and Canton walked into the Rampart trading post.

"What's up, boys?" Cap Mayo asked as they stepped up to the counter. "Ya look beat."

"Yeah? Well, we just finished with the log walls on the church building. We can maybe get the purlins and ridge log up in a day or two."

Cap nodded his head. "Sounds like ya are comin' right along. Heard Beach was helpin' ya."

"Yeah, he stopped by for a while. He's a good hand. But mostly, we came here to talk to ya about the miners' meeting. I'm ready to bring charges against the Swede."

Cap blinked a couple of times, looked from Coy to Canton, and then back to Coy. "You find yourself a witness?"

"We have a witness."

Cap nodded and said, "Well then, I reckon the next order of business is appointin' a sheriff. We don't have a regular one. We just appoint one as the need arises." Looking back at Canton he continued. "You're the most qualified person around. As mayor of Rampart, I hereby elect you. What say you?"

Canton nodded and said, "I accept."

"Well then, raise your right hand and say, 'I do'."

Canton raised his right hand and said, "I do."

Cap turned back to his register, opened it up, rummaged around in the back of the till, and pulled out a well-worn sheriff's badge. "Here. Better put this on to make it official."

As Canton pinned on the badge, Cap continued speaking. "I'll call a meeting for tomorrow at nine o'clock. Make sure your witness is here."

Canton smiled, and said, "Oh, he'll be here."

16

The Rampart trading post was doing a brisk business at eight forty-five the next morning when Coy arrived. Miners and prospectors crowded the front boardwalk as Coy worked his way to the entrance.

The temperature had fallen during the night, and a fog of breath hung in the lazy air above the crowd under the overhanging porch roof.

"Go get 'em, Preacher man," somebody encouraged.

"We're here for ya," another voice said.

Stepping inside, he quickly glanced around the warm, dim, pipe-and-wood-smoky interior.

Coy's attention was arrested by a group of men in animated conversation at the back counter. He saw Cap and Canton behind the counter and Duelin on the opposite side. To the right, with his arms folded and leaning against an upright support beam, stood the

Kid. The rest of Duelin's gang were scattered throughout the room.

Coy made his way to the counter while keeping his eyes on the Kid. The Kid's wandering gaze locked onto Coy's. The Kid stiffened, stood upright, and slowly lowered his hands to his side.

Coy locked eyes with Colorado and gave him a brief nod in acknowledgment as he continued to move up to the left side of Duelin. That placed Duelin between him and the Kid.

"Again, Mr. Duelin..." Cap was saying, "you're too late. We already have a duly appointed sheriff."

Duelin suddenly glanced to his left at Coy, and then across the counter at Canton, and then to his far right at the Kid. Picking up his papers from the counter top, Duelin huffed and pushed his way through the crowd toward Colorado.

"What was that about?" Coy asked.

Cap shook his head. "Oh, he had some papers with signatures claiming to make him the head of a vigilance committee and he wanted to make the Colorado Kid the acting sheriff. I told him he was a day late and a dollar short." Looking at Canton, he continued, "Shall we begin?"

Frank Canton stepped up on a bench and called for order in the trading post. As conversations died down, Canton stepped off the bench and gave Cap a hand taking his place.

"Boys!" Cap began, "It's been a while since the last meeting. For this to be done correctly, we need a chairman."

"I move that you be the chairman," somebody shouted.

"Second the motion," somebody else hollered.

The motion carried and Cap Mayo stepped down from the bench and sat at a table that had been cleared for him.

"Now, gentlemen. I need a clerk."

"I nominate Beach. He's right handy with a pen," somebody else suggested.

Again, it was seconded and passed. Beach came forward and pen and paper were provided to him.

Cap looked at Coy. "Preacher Coy Tucker, let's hear your story."

After stepping up to the table, Coy began.

"Thursday last, I determined to head up to the diggin's to introduce myself and invite the miners and prospectors who may not have heard that a minister of the gospel was available here in Rampart to church. I found the trail a little tougher than expected.

"At Miller Creek gulch, on the banks of Big Minook Creek, I made a small camp under a large spruce and reckoned on what I should do—continue or return to Rampart. During that time, I stepped out of my shelter and was assaulted. All I saw was a fist. All I heard before I blacked out was a voice. It was the Swede.

"When I came to, I spent the night under that shelter nursin' this shiner I'm sportin' and a raging headache where he kicked me. The next morning, I caught and ate some fish, and then, with the help of Mr. Miller and a few others who happened along, made it back to Rampart."

Cap looked over at Coy. "What did the voice say?"

"He said, 'The boss said not to kill ya'." Looking over at Duelin, he continued, "'But he didn't say nothin' bout workin' ya over some'."

Duelin's expression did not change.

"Well, there's no doubt you took a beatin'. Are ya sure it was the Swede and no one else?"

Coy turned his gaze to the crowd. He knew his accusation was weak. His only hope was whether Canton had persuaded Woolbright to testify about what he had seen. "I'm sure."

"Got any witnesses?" Cap asked.

Coy glanced around the room and saw a smile cross the faces of Duelin and the Kid. Everyone else stared at him, waiting for the answer. Looking at Canton, Coy made eye contact. Canton gave a slight nod. Looking at Cap he said, "I have."

"Bring him forward."

The smiles disappeared from Duelin and the Kid as they looked at Canton.

Canton turned and disappeared into Cap's living quarters. After some muffled conversation, he reappeared with Mr. Woolbright in the lead.

"Mister Woolbright, please tell this here committee what ya saw up on Minook Creek Thursday last, that has anything to do with these proceedings," Cap instructed.

"Well, sir," he began with a lowered voice.

"Speak up," someone shouted from the back of the room.

Woolbright looked at the floor, cleared his throat, and swallowed. Looking up and in a louder voice, he continued. "I was checkin' on a claim up Miller Creek that didn't pan out. On my way back to Rampart, about two o'clock or so, when I hit Minook Creek flats, I saw the Swede ahead of me on the trail, headin' downstream."

"You sure it was the Swede you saw?" Cap asked.

"Yes sir. It's hard to mistake the Swede, the way he walks."

A few snickers and some outright laughs erupted in the crowd.

Cap smiled and then said, "Well you're right there. So, what did ya' do then?"

"I hung back some. I wanted some distance between me and him."

"Thank ya, Mr. Woolbright. You may step down." Cap looked at the tabletop, pursed his lips, and nodded a couple of times.

Then, looking up at the crowd said, "So, we have an accusation it was the Swede, and we have a witness that places the Swede in that area at the right time. I reckon the next thing to do is call the Swede forward. Come on up here, Swede and tell your story."

Everyone looked around as a low murmur filled the room.

"He ain't here," someone in the back said.

"Canton, did ya notify him?" Cap asked.

"I notified everyone in town."

Cap turned to Duelin. "Where is he?"

Duelin scowled. "How should I know?"

"I saw him choppin' wood in front of his cabin earlier this mornin'," a voice volunteered.

Cap frowned and turned to Canton. "Take five men with ya and bring him here. In the meantime, I call a recess."

Then, with a louder voice said, "Somebody throw open 'em doors. It's gettin' a might close in here."

Coy watched Canton choose his posse and leave the building. A few miners gathered out on the boardwalk, while others stayed inside. Looking over at Duelin and the Kid sitting together at a table, Coy watched as Handshaker Bob joined them. Duelin whispered something to him, and then Handshaker Bob mingled with the crowd, stopping several times to briefly talk to people.

Cap turned to Coy and said, "Follow me."

Cap led him back into his living quarters and looked at Coy. Coy thought he detected worry on his face.

"I don't like the way this is goin'. We're gonna need more than that. Just 'cause ya say he did it, and just 'cause he was in the area, doesn't prove a thang. Although, him refusin' to come to the miners' meetin' does look suspicious. We need proof he was actually in your camp."

"Jehovah-Jireh."

"What's that?"

"The Lord will provide. Have faith."

Cap frowned and shook his head.

Cap Mayo led Coy to the meeting and sat down at his table. Five minutes later, a thumping sound and loud voices exploded from the front boardwalk. Men parted from the door as Canton and his posse escorted the Swede into the meeting at gunpoint. A loud murmur of voices erupted inside the meeting as well.

"Here's your man, Judge. As duly appointed sheriff, I have arrested the Swede on charges of assault." Holding something over his head, he continued, "Also found this here *Colt* New Line .22 in his pocket."

Cap banged his closed fist on the table. "Gentlemen, come to order. Looks like we've found our murderer, as well."

As the conversations and whispering died down, he continued. "The sheriff has arrested the Swede and accused him of assault on Preacher Coy Tucker. We'll deal with the possible murders separately if we get that far. He deserves a fair trial, and I appoint you, Buckskin Charlie, as his attorney. You have fifteen minutes to confer whilst I pick a jury."

As Buckskin talked with the Swede, Cap appointed a jury of twelve and positioned them along the wall to his right.

When completed, he turned to Buckskin Charlie. "Are you ready, Buckskin?"

"Yeah, we're ready."

Cap looked over at Beach. "Read the charge to the accused."

Beach stood and read the formal charge.

Addressing Buckskin and the Swede, Cap asked, "How do you plead?"

Buckskin replied, "Not guilty."

"Bring your witnesses, Sheriff."

Coy was called first and his story was repeated.

Buckskin was given the chance to question him, but he declined.

Woolbright was called next. Woolbright reluctantly came forward, it seemed to Coy. Woolbright glanced at the Swede. The Swede's face turned into a scowl. His eyes narrowed as he stared at Woolbright. Woolbright quickly looked at Mayo.

"Well, go on," Cap said. "You've already given your testimony once. It's in the record. Just do it again and pay no mind to that weasel."

Woolbright finally repeated his story, and no questioning from Buckskin could change it.

The Swede suddenly yelled, "Lies! All lies! I was nowhere up there, I tell ya." He stared hard at Woolbright as Woolbright left the stand and melted into the crowd.

Cap banged the table with his fist and said, "You shut your mouth, Swede. You'll have your chance."

Coy glanced over at Duelin and watched him cross his arms and glare at the Swede.

Then, something in the doorway caught Coy's attention. Looking more closely, he saw John Minook enter, take off his hat, and wave a hand to get Canton's attention. Canton made his way through the crowd to Minook. There, they talked for a few seconds.

"Now, do we have any more witnesses, other than the accused, to call before the court?"

As Cap finished asking his question, Canton made his way through the crowd and said, "I have one last-minute witness. I want to call John Minook to the stand."

The Swede suddenly stood. "He's a moose-hide. He ain't got no right here!"

Cap banged the table with his fist again. "Now, see here! Minook owns a claim on a creek that bears his name. I reckon he has as much, if not more of a right to be here than you do. Now. Sit. Down!"

The Swede slowly sat down.

Looking at Canton, Cap continued, "Sheriff, call your next witness."

Canton motioned Minook to come forward. Minook did so and stood by the table.

Cap made eye contact with him and said, "Tell us what ya know about this."

All eyes were on Minook. All was quiet.

And then he began.

"I come from claim on Little Minook. Cross Hunter Creek in flats by Miller Creek Gulch. Smell smoke... see small smoke under big spruce. Think maybe rest at white man camp. No one there. I look round some... see fish scraps... find small blood on bush. Find two white man's tracks in mud... boot tracks... one big... one smaller. Big one walk up behind spruce."

"Let me ask ya this Minook. Did ya see any other camps in the area?"

"No other camps."

"Okay. Now, do ya know who made those tracks?"

"Smaller ones, me no know. Bigger ones, Swede."

A low murmur spread through the room and then died down.

"Buckskin, do ya have any questions for the witness?"

"Yeah. How do ya know it was the Swede's tracks?"

Minook looked at Buckskin and nodded his head toward the Swede.

"Him big man. Walks with limp. Right foot drag... leave mark. No other track like Swede." Again, a low murmur and many heads nodded in apparent agreement.

Buckskin frowned. "No other questions."

Mayo nodded in response and said, "Thank you, Minook. Buckskin, the defendant can now give his story."

Buckskin conferred with the Swede in subdued tones. It appeared to Coy Buckskin did not like what the Swede was saying.

Turning to Cap, Buckskin said, "We decline."

Cap leaned back in his chair, looked around the room, and said, "Well, there ya have it, boys. We have testimony accusin' the Swede of assault. We have an eyewitness the Swede was in the area, and testimony placin' the Swede at the scene of the crime by way of evidence. That evidence being tracks left behind by the Swede, identified by Minook. We know Indians don't make mistakes readin' such sign."

Looking over at the jury, Cap continued. "It's now your job to decide if the Swede is guilty, or not. May I remind ya that the safety and lives of all concerned depend on your decision? It is customary, should ya find him guilty, for you, the jury to decide on punishment." Cap banged the table and said, "I now call a recess and you can confer amongst yourselves."

Five minutes after the jury went into a huddle, a verdict was reached. Cap Mayo called the meeting to order.

"Have you boys come to a decision?"

Old Freddy stepped forward. "We have. We all agree the Swede's not guilty."

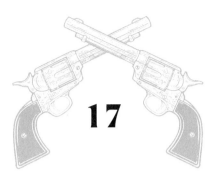

17

Murmuring and arguments instantly erupted in the trading post. Coy felt his heart sink. He halfway expected something like that to happen, however.

Cap banged his fists on the table.

Coy made eye contact with Duelin. He saw a smile, almost a sneer, cross Duelin's face. The kid was standing, poised, intently watching the crowd—ready for action.

"Order!" Cap yelled. "Order in this meetin'. Order!"

The clamor finally died down.

"Not guilty? Are ya out of your ever-lovin' minds?"

Old Freddy shuffled his feet and glanced at the others in the jury, and back at Cap.

"What we mean by that is... we can't tell, for sure, if the Swede done it or not." Quickly looking at the jury and then at Cap, he continued, "We uhm... that is, we the jury, believe this is a personal matter and should be worked out between the two."

Cap blinked a couple of times. "What do ya want? A shoot-out at noon on main street?"

"Oh, no, nothin' like that."

"Well... What?"

"Umm... A boxing match. At noon. On main, stree—"

The room instantly erupted in laughter. Coy watched a wide grin cross Duelin's face and the nod of approval he gave toward the jury. Duelin evidently had it figured that was as good as a 'not guilty' verdict.

Coy's gaze swung to the Swede. The Swede sported a grin. As he locked eyes with the Swede, memories of his younger days flooded his mind.

Memories of times past when he let anger get the better of him.

He felt a surge of adrenalin flood his veins as he thought to himself, *I am going to knock that grin off your face, big boy.*

The Swede's smile slowly faded and he turned his eyes from Coy.

"And then what?" Cap asked.

"The winner stays. The loser leaves on the river, without provisions, and never comes back."

The laughter suddenly stopped. The room became ghostly quiet. Everyone knew that that, in effect, was a death sentence.

A few minutes later in Cap's private residence, Coy sat at the kitchen table. Cap straddled the split-log bench with his left arm on the table, his right hand on his hip, and gave a big sigh as he studied the floor.

"Well, that was a surprise."

Margaret placed a cup of strong tea before each of them.

"Thank you," Coy said.

Margaret nodded in reply and walked to the stove. Cap didn't seem to notice she'd been there.

Coy took a sip of tea. Looking at Cap he said, "Not really. Thinkin' back on it, I should have seen it comin'."

Cap looked at Coy. "How so?"

Coy took another sip of tea and set his cup on the table.

"You were busy with the meetin' and all, so ya probably didn't see it. But during the hearing, Duelin sent his boys to mingle in the crowd. I believe he made threats that whoever was picked to be jurors, they were to find the Swede innocent. Canton told me that would probably happen. And, thinkin' back on it, that's exactly how Duelin got off the charges of cattle rustlin' back in Wyoming."

Cap shook his head and looked at the floor. "Why am I not surprised?" Looking back at Coy, he continued. "Look, I'll find some way to get a grubstake to ya somewhere downriver. Some of Minooks' relatives owe me a favor and—"

"Whoa, there hoss. What are ya talkin' about?"

Cap's eyes widened. "Surely ya can't... I mean, the Swede's a pretty big boy."

"The Swede's a bushwhacker. Likes to use his fists but doesn't like to face his mark. I saw that in his eyes. He, Duelin, and the rest of that outfit's got everybody buffaloed. Everyone's afraid of the Swede and that's what he's countin' on.

"It's time to call his bluff. He's not used to someone standin' up to him face to face. I've had my share of bar-room and back-street brawls. I think I can take him. Look...peace comes with a price. Ya have to fight for it. Win or lose, maybe I can inspire the rest of this community to stand up to Duelin and his gang."

Cap looked Coy up and down a couple of times, turned, picked up his cup, and downed half of its contents. Setting down the cup, he stared across the table at the wall and shook his head.

"Like I said, ya ain't like the others."

Just then, somebody knocked on Cap's door that led into the trading post. Margaret answered and let whomever it was into the living area.

Coy heard a voice ask, "Cap Mayo?"

Cap raised his head and said, "In here."

Footsteps approached and Rex Beach entered the kitchen area with his hat in his hands. "Um, the sheriff asked me to let you know they are almost ready. It will be held at the boat landing."

Cap nodded his head once and said, "Thank you."

Rex nodded in return, took a step backward, turned, and left—escorted out by Margaret.

As Coy made his way down the path to the water's edge, he saw, through the milling crowd, a boxing ring about twenty feet in diameter had been staked out with hemp rope, defining the boundaries. Coy stopped and surveyed the scene below.

Someone had hastily built a crude raft of logs pulled up on shore, for the loser.

Duelin, the Kid, and the Swede were grouped on one side of the ring. Canton and Beach stood on the other.

A group of men crowded around Hand-shaker Bob, who was taking cash and furiously writing in a book—evidently taking bets.

Coy knew the odds were against him. If the Swede won, Duelin would make some easy money. But what if the Swede lost?

Coy smiled to himself. Duelin would have a hard time covering those bets. Looking at his hands, he clenched his fists a couple of times. His hands felt stiff and leathery, and he smiled to himself again. He was glad he'd taken Beach's advice. His hands did not feel right for caressing a gun, but for working the land and working another man over, they would do.

In his mind, he prayed, *Father, give me strength over my enemies. Nevertheless, not my will, but Thine be done.*

Coy stepped into the ring and removed his coat, gun belt, and shirt. Those, he handed to Canton. Stretching his back and arm muscles, he felt the brisk air. He took in a deep breath, and it awakened a sense of consciousness—of vitality he had not experienced in a long while.

Cap stepped into the ring. "Boys, this is gonna be a bare-knuckles fight. The first one to go down and stays down for fifteen seconds is the loser. Any questions?"

"Any rules?" Canton asked.

"Oh, yeah. No hittin' below the belt. Now, does any of ya two have anythin' to say?"

"Yeah," the Swede growled, "Enough jaw-jackin'. Let's get on wid it."

"How 'bout you, Preacher?"

In a steady, even tone Coy said, "Mr. Swede, I've heard you're a two-bit, no-account thief and murderer. All I ask is that ya confess and ask forgiveness from God and those ya wronged."

"Or what, Preacher man?"

"Or, I will give ya a whippin'. Don't mistake my meekness for weakness."

"Ha! You're soft. You may be fast with a gun, but you're in my territory, now."

Coy slowly shook his head. "And you're a coward."

The Swede lunged fast from the rope with a growl, but Coy was faster.

Coy stepped to his left and flattened the corner of the Swede's lips with a looping left and followed with a hard right.

The move must have shocked the Swede because he blinked twice. Blood showed on his lips. But it did not stop him.

He plowed on, both arms flailing like the paddle of a stern wheeler. One punch rang bells in Coy's head, another caused sparks in his vision as Coy staggered back a step or two.

With a slight grin, the Swede came at him, but Coy had time to get set and, while rolling his shoulder, gave a hard left to the Swede's cheekbone.

That shook the Swede and put him in a daze.

Coy walked in—smashing left and right.

Blood ran from a cut on the Swede's cheekbone.

The crowd yelled, but to Coy, they, and the noise, seemed a long way off. Tunnel vision forced him to see only the big Swede.

The Swede gave a mighty shove.

Coy fell backward, landing hard. Coy saw a look of grim determination on the Swede's face as the big man came at him.

Coy came up fast, just in time to meet the Swede's hammering fists. Coy bobbed and weaved, trying to miss as many of the jarring blows as possible. The taste of blood came up in his mouth.

The Swede suddenly grabbed Coy with a mighty bear hug and began squeezing the breath out of him.

The smell of sweat, blood, and booze was thick in the close air.

Luckily, the Swede had only pinned Coy's left arm to his side. Cupping his right hand, Coy smacked the Swede's left ear—hard. The Swede howled and turned Coy loose. Grabbing his ear, the Swede grimaced, and bowed forward a bit.

Coy had broken the Swede's eardrum.

The Swede looked Coy up and down a couple of times, while still holding his left ear. His hairy, barrel chest, streaked with blood, heaved as he fought for breath.

The Swede's countenance seemed to change a little. It seemed to Coy a look—perhaps of fear—crossed the Swede's face.

Was Coy's assumption true? That the Swede had never had anyone stand up to him in a fair fight before?

A look of rage suddenly crossed the Swede's face. He ducked his head and charged.

Coy met his charge.

The Swede took a mighty swing at Coy's head.

Coy ducked and caught a glancing blow, that, nevertheless, made bells ring.

The momentum and power of the swing carried the Swede into a half turn and Coy smashed a left into the Swede's ribs.

The Swede stumbled a couple of steps and then turned to face his opponent.

Coy stepped in and gave a terrific right uppercut to the Swede's solar plexus.

A sick look crossed the Swede's face as he lost his wind and sank to all fours onto the sand and gravel of the Yukon River shore.

Coy stepped back then—both combatants gasping, fighting for oxygen.

"Come on, Swede," Coy said between gasps of air, "You're through... Admit what ya' done... and ask for forgiveness."

The Swede spat a gob of blood and saliva onto the rocks and sand between his hands.

"The blazes I will."

With that, the Swede began to rise.

Coy stepped in and dropped him with a hard right to the chin.

Canton counted out loud, "One... two... three... four..."

The Swede stirred, pushed himself to all fours, and struggled to stand up.

Coy stepped back to let him.

As soon as the Swede stood, Coy stepped in and planted a left and a right to the Swede's chin.

The Swede dropped like a burlap bag full of beans and he sprawled there for the full count.

18

Canton directed his five deputies to clear a path from the boxing ring to the raft lying at the water's edge.

Coy watched the proceeding as he mopped the sweat, spit, and blood from his face and upper body with his bandana. While doing so, he found a couple of open wounds he hadn't noticed. Not all the blood belonged to the Swede.

Cap Mayo unceremoniously dumped a bucket of cold Yukon River water in the Swede's face. He came to, sputtering and growling, ready to fight again.

"Hold on, there!" Cap demanded. "Fight's over. Let's go for a walk."

As Coy put his shirt on, Canton and Cap Mayo helped the Swede to his feet. The Swede stood there, swaying like an oak in a strong breeze as he looked around. The Swede and Bob Duelin locked eyes, and it seemed to Coy that a look of pleading crossed the Swede's face. Duelin shook his head with a look of disgust.

Coy thought to himself, *No honor among thieves, as they say*.

"Come on, Swede. Time to go," Canton said, as he turned him toward the river.

The Swede took two steps and then stopped and struggled. "No! I ain't goin'." Looking over his shoulder, he hollered, "Boss, don't let dem do dis to me. Duelin! Help me!!"

Canton drew his pistol and jammed it into the Swede's side. "You walk, or we'll drag your sorry carcass. Choice is yours."

Two deputies stepped up and all four bodily manhandled the Swede to the waiting raft.

There, the Swede fought harder. A fist from somewhere in the melee struck the Swede and he went out cold again.

The men laid him out on the raft and another bucket of water was dumped on his face. As he came to, they pushed the raft with a long slender pole into the current as far as they could.

The Swede sat upright and looked around. An upraised fist and a string of curses faded from sight and sound as the raft spun in the current amidst the pan ice and disappeared around the bend.

The mighty Yukon carried him into oblivion.

* * *

Bob Duelin looked around the crowd. A few people spoke to one another in hushed tones while glancing at him. He soon locked eyes with Coy Tucker, and a feeling of unease come over him.

"Let us go," he said to Colorado as he turned and headed up the path.

The Colorado Kid followed as they made their way to the North Star Saloon.

Inside, Duelin poured them both a drink, corked the bottle, and sat down, staring at the floor. The fight had taken an unexpected turn he was not ready for.

"What's wrong, Boss?"

Duelin glanced at the Kid, lightly shook his head, and looked at the floor. "As head of the vigilance committee, I should have said something in support of the verdict, condemning the Swede. I thought for sure the Swede would eat Coy's lunch."

The Kid took a sip and rested his left hand on the table, still holding the shot glass. "Well, at least the preacher did ya one favor. He got rid of one of your headaches for ya."

"A headachc I was willing to put up with. The Swede was also my scapegoat. Someone to pin the blame on when something happens to the preacher."

143

The Kid slowly rolled the shot glass between his thumb and middle finger. He suddenly stopped and looked into Duelin's eyes.

"*When* something happens? I thought you was gonna try to turn him. Bring him to your side."

Duelin took a sip of his drink for the first time and set it on the table. He twisted the shot glass in a circle a couple of times, reliving everything that had happened since the preacher's arrival.

"Preacher man Coy Tucker cannot be turned. I can see that now. Whether he is here, as you say, to take over and fleece the flock, or if he is legitimate, as he says, and wants to spread the gospel and bring law and order, I cannot tell. He is the proverbial thorn in my flesh, and he needs to be extricated. One way or another."

"You want I should call him out?"

Duelin swirled the amber liquid in his glass.

The Kid may be faster than the Preacher, and then again maybe not. I can not afford to lose the Kid. Besides, gunplay in the street would likely raise the ire of the camp. Especially now, after the fight. The Preacher had won it fairly.

It seemed the favorable sentiment he had successfully swayed away from the Preacher last Sunday services, was moving back to the preacher.

"No. It has to look like an accident."

* * *

Coy looked around at the crowd as he buttoned up his shirt and applied pressure to one of his face cuts with his bandana. Most everyone seemed to be in a somber mood.

It's never a pleasant thing to watch a man step off into eternity unprepared for the afterlife. To stand before his Just, and Holy Creator, defiant and unrepented. Nevertheless, that was the Swede's choice.

As Coy buckled on his twin *Peacemakers* he thought about Duelin and the Kid. He had watched them head uphill toward the North Star Saloon.

Duelin looked none too happy. He had evidently had his hopes dashed when the Swede lost. Coy was sure Duelin would now take more drastic measures.

That meant Coy's life was in greater danger.

Have I bitten off more than I can chew? Will my life also end here in the wilderness on the muddy banks of the Yukon?

Coy noticed movement in his peripheral vision and turned. Minook made his way through the crowd toward Coy.

"You come... My squaw fix you up. Make skookum tea... Hudson's Bay, willow bark tea... Plenty sugar. Help you heal."

"Much obliged." Coy looked at his stiff, swollen, and bleeding knuckles and clenched his fists a couple of times. "Guess I could use a little doctorin'."

As they approached John Minook's cabin, Coy was as impressed with its construction as he had been on his first visit.

It was built with squared, hand-hewn logs and dovetailed corner joints—cut close so nothing protruded past the outside corners. It looked nothing like the hastily built, ill-fitting saddle-notched logs so common in the mining camp.

Minook was skilled with his hands and spared no expense with its construction. At the front of the house was an enclosed entryway, made of whip-sawn lumber. Inside the entryway hung dog harnesses, gang lines, axes, saws, traps, and other items needed for daily life in the sub-arctic wilderness.

Stepping from the entryway into the cabin, Coy quickly glanced around. A woman about Minook's age worked by the cook stove. She wore a cotton trade dress and a light-colored cotton blouse. A shawl covered her jet-black hair.

As she worked, she stole a glance at Coy and quickly looked away. Two young girls and a younger boy sat on a bunk to Coy's left. The youngsters shyly stared at him. A puppy worried a bone on the whip-sawn wood floor. All in all, the cabin was neat and clean with everything in its place.

Minook looked at Coy and pointed to a washbasin with hot water already poured. Minook said something in Athabaskan to the older woman.

Looking at Coy he said, "My woman... She make tea."

As he washed up, Coy gingerly felt his face, probing for sore spots. Looking into the mirror, he saw his face was puffy. The cut over his left eye had stopped bleeding. The one on his right cheekbone still oozed a bit.

Coy sat at the table. Mrs. Minook brought him a cup of Hudson's Bay and willow bark tea. Coy took a sip. It was bitter.

The look on Coy's face must have been funny because Minook laughed out loud.

Minook pushed a tin box across the table to Coy. "Sugar... Plenty sugar."

Coy heard the girls snickering on the bunk.

"Like you said, Minook, skookum tea."

Coy added four teaspoons full of sugar and gave it another try. Then, he added two more.

The tea was still a little bitter but tolerable and felt good going down.

Mrs. Minook brought over a small tin of salve and applied the salve to the cuts on his face.

"What's this? Smells like spruce trees."

"Spruce sap and bear fat... Make cuts heal faster. You take... Use ever day."

Mrs. Minook finished applying the salve, left the opened tin on the table, and returned to the stove.

Coy took a couple more swallows of tea and picked up the tin. He sniffed it a couple of times.

"That smells pretty good. Will it work on my hands? My knuckles, I mean?"

Minook nodded once.

Coy was touched by Minook's generosity. Already the pain in his face had subsided. Whether it was the willow bark tea, the salve, or both, he did not know. "I'll pay ya for the doctorin' and the salve. Or trade... whichever."

Minook waved his hand as if brushing away a mosquito. "What I do, I do for Creator."

A serious look came over Minook's face and it seemed to Coy that perhaps Minook wished to discuss something.

"Somethin' on your mind, Minook?"

Minook glanced at his wife in the kitchen and made eye contact with her. Then, he looked back at Coy.

"My woman... Cap Mayo's woman... They talk. All young mans come back from huntin... Get plenty moose. Maybe we help build church... Maybe church chase all bad mans away... Bring peace."

Coy was mildly surprised and touched by the offer. At that time, though, he wasn't sure about anything in his life. Doubts and double guessing creeped into his thoughts.

"I don't know Minook. I've been here a week, and this is the second time I've taken a beatin'. And I was just healin' up pretty good from the last one. I won this fight, yes, but at what price? The life of another? Minook, there's always going to be bad men, ya know that. There's bad men amongst your own people. I once was a bad man. I still have bad dreams about some of the things I done. Who am I to try to make a difference?"

Minook looked at the tabletop for a few seconds, and then back at Coy. Minook nodded his head a couple of times.

"Plenty bad mans... More plenty good mans. You good man now. Bad, good, all need church. Creator say build church... You build church."

19

His nightmares had returned, only this time something was different. Flames again. That's what he remembered. But this time he was in the midst of them. He remembered looking around and realizing he was in a sanctuary of some sort. He unexpectedly saw someone's lower torso lying behind a pulpit, face down.

Who is that?

Thinking the person needed help, Coy moved forward. The flames abruptly leapt toward him.

Coy woke with a start. With difficulty and involuntary grunting, he rolled over and propped himself up on one elbow. His upper body was sore from overexerting himself during the fight.

Coy rubbed his eyes and shook his head, trying to clear his mind. He briefly wished he had Mrs. Minook's bitter willow bark tea for his aches and pains.

Perhaps strong hot coffee will work.

Reaching over to the little Yukon stove with stiffened and swollen hands, he fumbled open the door and raked through the ashes with the poker, looking for live coals.

He found a few, and those he raked into a pile. On top of the coals, he added a handful of spruce twigs and then a few sticks about the size of a shovel handle.

Coy lightly blew on the smoking twigs and they erupted into flames. He added three larger pieces of stove wood and left the stove door open to provide light.

In the soothing heat, Coy rose and stretched his stiffened muscles. Gingerly feeling his face, he reckoned it didn't feel too swollen.

He dressed, lit the coal oil lamp, and fixed his breakfast.

While eating, he opened his Bible, closed his eyes, and laid a stiff finger on the page, as was his habit. Whatever passage he laid his finger on, he read and thought about.

With breakfast and morning meditation over, Coy stepped out of his tent and raised his collar against the cold.

Below his land, in the fast-growing mining camp, diffused yellow light softly glowed through tents and frosted windows of log buildings.

A fog of wood smoke hung in the still air as morning breakfast fires were lit.

With a coffee cup in hand, he took a few steps around the corner to look over the work accomplished on the church building.

The sun peeked over the horizon in the southeast, over the hills of the Rampart mining district. The early morning light gave a bluish tint to the scattered paper birch's trunks. The shadows of the spruce were cloaked in chocolate brown.

Through the tree trunks, Coy saw a bright yellow horizon, streaked with clouds, fading upward into a reddish-orange glow. Behind the clouds, a blue-gray sky showed through at intervals and finally gained prominence above the cloud bank.

The temperature had dropped over night, and it seemed to Coy that was the coldest it had been since his arrival. A feeling of urgency about completing the construction overcame him.

Canton and Beach had helped him get the walls to eave height, but he knew it had taken time away from their mining. Canton had recently purchased claim thirteen above discovery on Julia Creek, and Coy was sure he was anxious to prove it and start sinking a shaft.

Coy looked over the log structure again.

Well, it's not going to finish itself, he decided, as he took another swig of coffee.

The coffee was lukewarm and he wrinkled his nose as he swallowed. Tossing the rest of the contents on the ground, he turned and headed into the tent.

Coy was bent over, just finishing the first cut through the logs of one side of what would be the front door, when he heard voices coming from the other side of his tent.

As he stood upright, a muscle spasm shot through his back between his shoulder blades. He involuntarily grunted and stretched his back and arm muscles. They seemed not quite as stiff as they had earlier, but nevertheless sore.

His hands and knuckles, however, were still swollen. They had taken the brunt of the punishment. Coy hoped he wouldn't have to quickly draw his weapon any time soon.

Stepping around the tent, he saw a group of people coming up the hill toward him. In the lead were Minook with his and Cap's wives, followed by all their children. Several miners, three or four white women, their children, and a few other Indians made up the rest of the group.

Minook walked up to Coy and said, "We make potlatch... Help build... Womans, they make food... Moose head stew. Have plenty rice. You have plenty dried vegetables?"

Coy was a little taken aback. "Um, yes. Plenty of dried vegetables."

"Good. They set up cooking pot... Build fire. We work. Cap Mayo, he come later tonight."

Minook turned and walked to his wife.

A tall, well-built bearded man, about the same size as Coy, stepped forward, took off his hat, and stuck out his hand. "They call me Chilkoot Charlie."

Coy took his hand and shook it. "I'm Coy."

"Yes-sir. I um..." He glanced at an Indian woman who stood behind him. Looking at Coy he continued, "That is, my wife and me want to apologize for doubting you last Sunday. We're mighty proud to see somebody finally standing up to Duelin and his gang."

Looking at the others, he turned back to Coy and said, "We're in mighty need of some spiritual guidance around here, so we're here to help finish with the building and maybe get ya moved in today."

A lump rose in Coy's throat. "Well thank ya, Chilkoot. Means a lot. And welcome. You ram-rodin' this outfit?"

"No sir. You are, but I'll get 'em movin' in the right direction, if need be."

Coy studied him a moment. Chilkoot met him eye to eye and never wavered. Coy saw honesty and humbleness there.

"With a moniker like 'Chilkoot', ya must've been around awhile."

"Was one of the first to climb over in ninety-six, before there was a Klondike rush. Made and lost a fortune. Built a cabin or two in the process."

"Good enough. Get with me in a few minutes in the tent and we'll go over some ideas. And thank ya, again."

Chilkoot nodded once, replaced his hat, and returned to his wife.

Coy looked around and noticed Beach among the crowd. Coy made his way to him. "I just wanted to thank ya for all your help."

Beach shrugged. "No problem. Not like I had anythin' else to do."

"Seen Canton around?"

"Yeah, saw him this mornin'. Said he was headin' up to his claim for a few days."

"I kinda figured he would. Also figured you'd be wantin' to get back to workin' yours."

Beach smiled. "Tell ya the truth, that claim's a dud. Oh, there's enough to make pay, but barely, so I've been workin' on another project. But right now, I'm kinda stuck. Gotta do some thinkin' on it."

"What kind of project?"

"A novel. I fancy someday I'll get it published."

Coy was mildly surprised. "A novel huh? What's it about?"

Beach shrugged and looked at the half-breed and white children playing together and then smiled. "Prejudices, basically."

"Sounds interestin'. I'd like to read it someday. Whatcha gonna call it?"

Beach looked at Coy. "The Barrier."

Coy thought a bit. "You know, prejudice has been with us a long time. Ever since Cain and Able. Cain bein' a farmer and Able a sheep herder. We all harbor and have been victims of prejudice in one form or another. It's not just about race. And, I do agree we need to break down some of those barriers."

Beach's eyes widened a little. "Ya know, you've given me some things to think about. Thanks."

"Well, it's just my two cents' worth. I look forward to readin' it. Now, if you'll excuse me, I have to talk with Chilkoot."

Inside the tent, Coy found Minook and Chilkoot discussing the building project. Coy let out another grunt as he sat cross-legged on the ground by the stove and held his hands to the heat.

Looking at the other two he said, "Thanks, boys, for the help. I don't think I would have gotten it done before the big snows come. You see how far me, Beach, and Canton got? All I need to do now is put a roof on her and a floor. Maybe a platform up front to put a pulpit on. Let me warm up my hands a little and I'll finish sawin' out the door."

"No... You stay... We work."

Coy looked at Minook and wondered what he meant by that.

"Um..." Chilkoot began, "We think ya should take it easy for a couple more days. You know, heal up? Do some studyin' or somethin'...whatever."

Coy looked from one to the other. "I can't do that, boys. I gotta be out there makin' sure everything gets done."

"No... You tell us... We do."

Coy clenched his teeth as he stared at Minook. It went against his grain to have someone tell him what to do. Old feelings of mistrust surfaced.

Is there an ulterior motive, or are they genuinely concerned about my well-being?

Minook's gaze did not waver.

"My squaw, she doctor you... Make feel better. We need skookum Preacher man."

Coy looked at Chilkoot Charlie.

Charlie met Coy's gaze and nodded his head twice.

Well, it is true I need some rest.

There were only a handful of men in Coy's life he felt he could trust.

Minook is one of them, he decided, *and Chilkoot seems an all-right fellow...*

Looking at Minook, Coy said, "Well, I can see there ain't no winnin' this argument."

20

Bob Duelin took another puff on his cigar. He stood outside the saloon tent and peered up the hill at the flurry of activity. The construction of the church building seemed to be quickly moving along. Of course, with that many people working on it, it should.

Duelin glanced to his left at the construction of the North Star Saloon and tightened his jaws. His workers seemed slow compared to those on the hill. It had taken his workers at least two months to get it framed and closed in. And still, there were a few last-minute details to tend to before it would be completed. He wanted it finished before the grand opening in a week.

Duelin looked up the hill.

How much is Coy paying them to work like that?

Duelin and his bartender inventoried North Star's stock and marked each bottle's fluid level with a grease pencil. Movement at the tent flap caught Duelin's attention. Looking up, he watched Handshaker Bob enter.

"Ya see all the commotion goin' on up the hill?" Bob asked as he removed his coat.

Duelin turned his attention to his inventory ledger and said, "Could not miss it. The preacher sure picked a fine place to build. Now he shall always be looking down his nose at me... I suppose they will be finished in a day or two."

Bob pulled out a chair and sat at a tables. "My aunt Nellie's brazier. Talk is, they'll be done by tonight. They're puttin' a steeple up right now."

Duelin sighed and said, "Tonight, huh?"

"Yep. The siwash are gonna have a dedication potlatch or somethin' when they're done."

So, Preacher man Tucker is in good with the Indians, now, Duelin thought to himself. *With all the activity up there, it seems a lot of whites I scared off last Sunday are siding with Coy, as well. It's time for action.*

"Speaking of meetings, we will have ours a little early today. Round everyone up and be back here in thirty minutes. We shall meet in the new building."

Thirty minutes later, Duelin paced back and forth on the new North Star Saloon's stage. The wood stove threw off a good amount of heat, and the warmed newly sawn wood gave off a clean, woodsy turpentine scent.

Although he owned a bar, he seldom drank what he peddled. Now, however, he downed his second shot.

Every event that had happened since Coys' arrival went through Duelin's mind, and it irked him to think everything he did only seemed to work in Coy's favor.

He had glanced up the hill as he had made his way to the new saloon, and sure enough, there was a steeple on the church building. Someone had even found enough white paint to paint it.

Duelin heard the door open, and he glanced at it as he continued to pace. The Colorado Kid, followed by Handshaker Bob, Camp Robber Freddy, The Blueberry Kid, the bartender, and the Faro dealer came into the room and stood in front of the stage. Duelin continued to pace.

"Boys, we are going to have our grand opening tonight in the new building. Spread the word.

"While everyone is here, having a grand time, I need a volunteer to give preacher man Tucker a little visit. We need to get rid of him. Torch the building, and make it look like an accident. If he is permitted to stay, everything we've worked for will be for naught."

The gang members glanced at each other.

Duelin noticed and stopped his pacing. "What? You got something to say?"

They glanced at each other again.

The Blueberry Kid spoke up. "Everything *we've* worked for? The only thing we've worked for is you... And you take half of what we get."

Duelin tightened his jaws, took a deep breath, and said, "And you, in return, get protection."

"Protection? The Swede didn't get much protection."

Duelin directly faced them. "I fixed the jury. They found him not guilty. I even had them decide to have them duke it out because I figured the Swede would beat Coy's brains out. How was I supposed to know that preacher knew how to fight?"

Colorado cleared his throat and said, "Boss, I warned you a couple o' times, he ain't nothin' to mess with. You're pokin' a bear with a stick. And besides, you're talkin' murder here. Ain't none of your crew, except the Swede, has ever killed a man."

"You have."

"All the men I've killed were shootin' back. I am not a dry-gulcher. If and when the time comes to face the preacher, it will be on equal terms. I owe him that much."

Duelin lost self-control and hurled his shot glass at the wall. It shattered and everyone ducked the glass shrapnel.

"You passel of cowards. NO! This is my town. I run it. The preacher man cannot stay... Even if I have to burn him out myself. Now, get out of my sight."

* * *

Coy was lost in his reading, but a sound of rustling at the front of the tent made him turn and look.

Minook poked his head into the tent. "You come now... See."

Coy laid his bible aside, rose, and checked his watch. It read five fifteen. He had lain around all day and the rest had done him good. He felt much better.

Putting on his long black coat and hat, he stepped out of the tent. The children danced and chased each other around him as he walked to the church building. At his first view of the building, the lines of the walls led his eyes to the slope of the roof. Which, in turn, led his eyes up the tall, slender, white steeple to the point—which disappeared into the heavens. Behind the church and to the right, stood a proper log cache on stilts.

A lump arose in his throat.

Minooks' wife, smiling, and standing by the porch, pointed at the door, "Come... See."

Coy stepped up on the porch and entered through the door. It squeaked on its wooden hinges.

A wax candle rubbed on the hinge pins will fix that.

Inside, two windows covered in waxed parchment, one on each side of the building, provided light. In the center of the sanctuary stood a wood stove.

At the front of the sanctuary they had built a platform. On it rested a pulpit unlike any Coy had ever seen. Someone had found a twelve-inch spruce tree with two large burls growing about a foot and a half from each other. They completely encircled the trunk. The bottom burl was cut straight across to sit upright on the platform. The top burl was cut across at a slight angle to provide a flat sloping area to rest his open bible on.

In front of the pulpit sat a small table with two coal-oil lamps to provide light.

Behind the platform and pulpit, they had built a partition with a door.

Walking through the door, Coy found a room eight feet by as wide as the building. It would be his private quarters.

Stepping back into the sanctuary, he looked at everyone gathered. He was touched by their outpouring of love and generosity. Each, in their way, gave of their time and talent to the lord.

With a lump in his throat and genuine humbleness, he did the best he could to thank them all without choking up. He promised to do his best to lead them in all spiritual matters.

Minook stepped forward. "We make potlatch now."

The women left and soon returned with trade blankets, and moose, and caribou robes. The women placed the materials on the wooden floor, surrounding the wood stove. The guests sat on the blankets and robes.

The Indian men carried in a big pot of moose-head soup with vegetables and rice and placed it next to the stove.

Other food items were brought in, as well. Bannock, smoked and grilled salmon, mashed highbush cranberries, mixed with plenty of trade sugar, and copious amounts of strong black tea, rounded out the feast. All was served on birch-bark dishes.

When supper was over and the extra food put away, Minook's crew brought out their drums. Dancing and singing in the Athabaskan language followed for half an hour. Minook interpreted to Coy what the songs meant.

The first songs were 'sorry songs'—songs about those who had passed on before. Then, 'new songs' were sung to give thanks to Minook for sponsoring the potlatch. Next, songs to give thanks to Coy for the spiritual guidance they expected.

A few of the miners slipped out and soon returned with fiddles and a guitar. One even had a harmonica. When the Indians were done, the miners tuned up and played a mixture of down-home mountain music and gospel.

Coy was surprised to learn most of the Indians were familiar with the fiddle. Their people had heard fiddle music since the early 1800s when voyagers and Hudson's Bay men worked their way into the eastern part of the territory of Alaska. Some of their people, they said, even knew how to play the fiddle.

Coy noticed Minook lean over and whisper something to his oldest daughter. She, in turn, whispered to her sister and Cap Mayo's kids, and they all left the building. They returned with Cap in the lead, each carrying a flour sack slung over their shoulder, stuffed full of... something.

Minook stood up and raised his hand. The room became quiet as the guests realized he was asking for silence.

The crowd moved back and made a circle around the room. In the center, Mayo and the kids opened their flour sacks and dumped blankets, knives, furs, snowshoes, bolts of calico cloth, cooking utensils, and beaded smoke-tanned garments. The latter included jackets, vests, moccasins, gloves and beaver fur mittens, and gun cases.

Cap walked toward Coy and stood by him as Minook addressed the crowd.

Coy looked at Cap. "What's going on?"

Cap smiled and tilted his head toward Coy while watching the crowd.

"Gift-givin' time. Minook, the host, gives away gifts to all attendees, for thanks and to cement his prestige as a leader and provider to his people. Kind of a redistribution of wealth. It also shows loyalty and friendship to the rest of us. By the way, heard tell the steamer *P.B. Wear* was at Tanana yesterday. She should be in sometime tonight or early in the mornin'."

"Well, that's good news. Maybe she'll have enough bacon and beans to get us through the winter."

Cap frowned. "Maybe. Problem is, she's loaded with stampeders, too. Some will get off here, others will probably try for Fort Yukon. I noticed more pan ice on the river today. Figure two weeks at the most before freeze up."

They both fell silent then, as they turned their attention to the festivities. Minook handed out gifts to all in attendance—even to the children, who received candy, a rare commodity in the wilderness.

Last, of all, Minook brought to Coy a beaded and fringed, smoke-tanned moose-hide jacket, neatly folded into a bundle. On top rested a pair of beaver fur mittens with beaded moosehide cuffs.

"My wife... She make for you."

Coy took the bundle in his left hand and examined the items, tracing the outline of the beaded floral design with his right forefinger, admiring the fine, intricate needlework. At the same time, he struggled to maintain his composure and tried to think of a way to express his deep gratitude.

Finally, he said, "Tell your wife my heart is full. I will wear them with pride."

Minook looked pleased as he nodded once and turned to leave.

Later, after Coy once again thanked everyone for their generous voluntary work on the building, and after the gifts and the instruments were packed in their cases, and as everyone began to leave for their own homes, Coy offered Minook his help carrying their supplies. As he did so, he saw Chilkoot approach.

"Preacher, while you're gone, I wanna sand the top of that pulpit one more time. Tomorrow

I'll put a coat of shellac on her if that's okay."

"Sure. I'll be back in a half hour or so."

* * *

Duelin stuck a pistol in his front waistband and, with a drink in his hand, staggered out of the new North Star Saloon. He weaved a little as he looked up the hill.

He had lost a lot of business during the grand opening of the new saloon because of that preacher man. Half of the mining camp, it seemed, was up there. The rest of the camp evidently chose not to patronize his establishment.

Oh, there were the usual drunks looking for a free drink, but that was it. The Faro dealer sat idle. The bartender could only polish glasses so many times. The only job the barkeep had was keeping Duelin's glass full of liquid courage.

Duelin quickly realized everyone seemed to be leaving the church building. He waited and watched as he took another sip of the amber liquid.

Yes. Yes, they are all leaving. Maybe they will stop in now, he thought.

As the crowd advanced down the main street, they dispersed to their own homes.

"What?" he yelled. "You too good to stop by my establishment?"

Several people glanced over at him. He knew they could see the gun in his waistband.

"Just because you built a church doesn't mean nothing. You all think you're better than me? You bunch of cowards. Haven't I helped you when you needed it? Didn't I warn you about the preacher man and who he really is? Huh? Didn't I?"

The crowd passed on by in silence. No one stopped.

Bob Duelin stood there all alone.

Turning, he looked up the hill and then tossed back the rest of his drink and swallowed.

"Now's the time," he said out loud. "No one there but the preacher."

21

Coy made his way from Minook's cabin down the street toward the trader's store. As he passed the North Star Saloon, he briefly remembered Duelin's tirade as they passed by earlier. It seemed obvious to him and probably everyone present that Duelin was losing control. In whispered voices, they said no one had ever seen him act that way before. Duelin had exposed himself to the rest of the camp for what he was—a common thug with his own interests in mind.

At the path by Mayo's trading store that led up to the fourth bench, the dancing, weaving north lights caught Coy's attention. He stopped, turned, and looked across the Yukon at the northern sky.

The clouds had completely dissipated, and it was the first time he had seen the Aurora clearly, in all their glory. He stood, mesmerized as they grew higher and higher overhead.

Soon, a ribbon of green light broke away, curling and twisting, heading south.

Coy turned to watch as it snaked above the church building, and then disappeared behind the steeple and hills beyond. Coy smiled at the thought of the beauty and wonder of it all.

Coy suddenly realized there was a dancing yellow light shining through the waxed parchment windows, much brighter than the glow from a coal-oil lamp. Fear gripped him, as it does with anyone who lives in a log structure in the northland. The fear of uncontrolled fire.

"Fire... FIRE!" he yelled, as he sprinted up the path. "FIRE!"

As he rounded his tent, a figure opened the door from the inside and stepped out. Because of the black-lit glow, Coy could not make out a face. But from what he could see, it seemed as though the man wore a mask.

The figure stood there, legs apart, and pulled something out of his waistband.

Coy's brain screamed, *GUN!* He dove to the ground as a bullet angrily whined past his head.

Coy rolled over and somehow his *Peacemaker* was in his hand. He threw a shot at the figure in the doorway and saw him flinch.

The figure turned and ran, disappearing in the night shadows.

Coy got his feet under him and sprinted to the door. By now, smoke rolled out the doorway and fell upward into the cold night air. He saw flames on the floor, licking at the small table in front of the pulpit, and the broken coal-oil lamps lying in the flames.

Through those flames, on the platform and behind the burl pulpit, he saw a body covered in blood, lying face down.

That must be Chilkoot.

Coy holstered his gun. *How am I going to get him out?*

The memory of the Buffalo Soldiers burning to death years ago surfaced in his brain and he shuddered. It was his actions that caused their deaths. Being burned alive surely was the worst way to go.

The heat was intense and Coy stepped back, raising both hands to shield his face.

If I die in these flames, it's what I deserve, Coy thought. *But what about Chilkoot? Maybe he's already dead. But what if he's not? He doesn't deserve to die. Not like this.*

Coy burst through the flames.

Turning the body over, Coy saw Chilkoot's eyes roll and knew he was still alive.

"Stay with me. I gotcha."

With a mighty tug, Coy rolled Chilkoot into his arms, gritted his teeth, and pushed the floor away from himself with his feet as he stood up.

Coy turned, took a deep breath of smoky air, and briskly walked through the flames. The heat was intense, and the exposed skin of his face and hands felt as if they were being seared in a hot skillet. As he emerged, he exhaled the acrid air from his lungs and uncontrollably coughed.

Cap rushed through the door, followed by Beach and a couple of others.

"You all right? That Chilkoot? Anybody else in here? He alive?"

Coy didn't answer but continued coughing as he pushed his way outside, knelt, and laid Chilkoot on the ground. Looking back at the church building, he realized there was no saving it. The flames rolled out of the doorway with the smoke. Tendrils of smoke rose from the roof here and there, indicating flames would soon take their place.

Men soaked Coy's tent with water to keep it from spontaneously combusting in the intense heat.

With his coughing under control, Coy looked at Chilkoot. He saw and smelt Chilkoot's singed hair still smoking.

"Did you see who did this?"

Chilkoot rolled his eyes. Through ragged breaths, he said, "D... Duelin. Knifed me... good."

Coy looked back at the burning building.

So, that's where all the blood came from. And there had been a lot of it on the platform.

His attention returned to Chilkoot.

Chilkoot had closed his eyes. His breath came in short, rapid succession. Coy knew Chilkoot would not make it through the night.

Chilkoot's Indian wife pushed her way through the crowd, wailing. She fell on him there, and held him, rocking back and forth, sobbing.

Chilkoot shuddered and then softly groaned as his soul left its earthly body.

* * *

Bob Duelin pulled off his mask and staggered in the dark through the brush and trees along the bench until he was behind the North Star Saloon.

There he waited, watching his back trail.

Is anyone following? Probably not. Everyone's attention is on the church.

When he stepped out of the building and saw the preacher racing toward him, it stunned him. Who had he just killed? The only thing he could think to do was shoot at Coy to give himself time to get away.

Duelin looked down at his leg. It worked, but not without a cost.

Too bad that another fellow was there instead of the preacher. He had not counted on that. He could have sworn it was the preacher when he snuck up behind him and knifed him in the kidney.

He smiled then. *At least the building is a total loss. The body and any other evidence will be destroyed. The fire sure gives out a bright glow in the night sky.*

A twinge in his right thigh demanded his attention. The shock of the bullet wound, as well as the alcohol haze was wearing off. The once dull pain was intensifying. His pant leg felt sticky. He knew it was blood. His blood.

Taking a step, he stumbled and almost fell. Duelin looked around and found a dead branch to use as a walking stick. With it, he turned and worked his way downhill.

As he reached the back of his building, the roaring and crackling of the church fire caught his attention and he looked up the hill.

Sparks shot from the flames into the night sky like fireworks. The reflected light the inferno gave was enough for him to pick his way through the scrap lumber lying around and make it to the front of the saloon.

He peaked around the corner. The street was empty. Everyone, it seemed, was up the hill. Duelin limped around the corner and pushed his way inside.

No one was there.

Where are they, those cowards?

He stumbled once as he worked his way behind the bar and grabbed a bar rag. Sitting down on a chair, Duelin inspected the bullet wound. It had just grazed his thigh, cutting a neat grove in his skin. He tightly tied the rag around the wound, attempting to staunch the blood flow, and then poured himself another drink.

Duelin heard sudden noises on the boardwalk at the door. He was edgy.

Is the preacher coming for me? He pulled his gun and pointed it at the door.

The door swung open and in stepped the Colorado Kid. The Kid hesitated as he looked Duelin up and down, and then sneered at him. As the Kid shut the door he said, "Put that away before ya hurt yourself."

Duelin stuck the gun in his waistband. "I almost shot you."

"In your condition, you would've missed, and that would've been the last thing ya almost done."

Duelin looked him up and down. The Kid seemed to be in a bad mood. "What are you so surly about?"

"Well, ya done it, now. The whole camp's turned against ya. Camp Robber Freddy mingled with the crowd up there. Seems as though the miner you stabbed lived long enough to tell 'em who done it." Colorado nodded at Duelin's leg. "And that bullet wound marks you as the man. The preacher's comin' for ya, Mr. Duelin. Make no mistake."

Panic and fear welled inside Duelin. "You and me. We can take him. We could set up a trap, see, and when he comes in..."

Colorado shook his head. "I done told ya before, I don't fight like that. I'm not a coward. I face my enemy. No, you're on your own, Boss. There ain't no winnin' this one. If by chance ya do get Caleb, or the preacher as ya call him, ya still have the camp to face. There's no place to hide."

Colorado turned to leave.

Duelin felt anger boil up inside, replacing the fear. He gritted his teeth and grabbed for his gun.

Colorado drew, cocked his *Smith and Wesson*, and spun to face Duelin in one fluid move.

Duelin was caught with his gun halfway out of his pants. He froze.

Colorado smiled. "No. No, I'll not shoot ya. I'll leave that to the preacher."

With his gun still pointed at Duelin, Colorado backed to the door, holstered his gun, and quickly slipped out.

* * *

Coy pulled the hammer back on his *Peacemaker* to half-cock, flipped open the loading gate, and replaced the spent cartridge with a fresh round. Turning the cylinder until the empty chamber was under the hammer, he closed the loading gate and gently lowered the hammer. He now had five live rounds in each *Colt*.

"Better let Canton take care of Duelin. I can re-appoint him as sheriff."

Coy turned toward the voice and eyeballed Cap.

Turning back, he twirled the *Peacemaker* a couple of times and thrust it into his holster. Looking back at Cap he said, "Canton ain't here," and he began to walk away.

"We ain't got no choice. Canton is the closest thing we have for a lawman. Besides, ya ain't in the right frame of mind."

Coy stopped and faced him.

Cap's eyes grew wide.

"Just what frame of mind do I have to be in? We have another killer in our community. He'll kill again. If not me, then somebody else. You speak of choices. I'm the next best thing ya got, and I choose to do this. I'll bring him back alive if I can. If not, I'll bring him back dead. *That* choice is his."

179

22

Duelin pushed himself out of the chair. His right leg felt a little stiff and throbbed with pain. He had moved his belongings to an upstairs room the day before and decided to go there to find some headache powder and possibly get much-needed sleep.

Reaching the top of the stairs, Duelin opened the door of the biggest room he called the suite. Hearing a noise downstairs, he turned and looked down to the first floor.

The front door of the saloon swung open. No one entered.

Duelin furrowed his brow, thinking. *The preacher! It must be him.*

Duelin stood beside the upstairs railing support post, drew his gun, and waited. He realized to late, he had not reloaded when he fired at the preacher earlier.

"Duelin! Give yourself up peaceful like. You'll get a fair trial. Cap Mayo's here with me as a witness."

Duelin saw Coy poke his head around the edge of the doorpost. It was what he was waiting for. Duelin threw a quick shot and blew splinters off the door post above Coy's head.

The sound of the gunshot reverberated inside the building and Duelin's ears rang. He grimaced at the pain and held his left hand over his ear—too late to do any good.

"You have ruined me, Coy Tucker. You are the reason for all my troubles. I should have gotten rid of you sooner. Come and get me, if you have the guts."

Coy barged through the door and threw himself to the side, toward the end of the rough plank bar.

Duelin was ready and threw another shot. It seemed to Duelin, Coy's coat flew back a little.

Did I hit him? Possibly. I don't think he knows for sure where I am.

Duelin watched from the support post of the upstairs balcony railing. He soon saw Coys' eyes peer over the bar, apparently searching for him. Their eyes locked and Duelin fired another round as Coy's head disappeared behind the bar.

Duelin scurried behind another support post, further along the balcony railing, closer to the opposite end of the bar from where Coy hid. He could barely see Coy's shoulder.

Two rounds left, he figured.

"Duelin! Give yourself up. I don't want to have to kill you. Don't make me do this."

"Come and get me, preacher man."

Coy stood and aimed at where Duelin had been. Then, Duelin saw Coy turn toward him—his long black coat swirled outward as he turned.

Duelin fired and Coy fired—the two shots sounded almost like one.

Duelin saw dust fly from Coy's long black coat. He also felt something like a fist hit him in the chest. The impact made him hunch a bit. Curiously, he saw gun smoke lazily curling upward from the end of Coy's gun barrel.

A darkness in his peripheral vision slowly worked its way to the center.

Total darkness replaced sight as the sensation of falling, falling, and endless falling and heat overcame him.

"Y'all right, preacher?"

Coy looked over at Cap. "Yeah, I think so."

Coy shoved the *Peacemaker* into its holster and heavily sighed as he looked at Duelin's twisted body lying on the floor in front of the stage.

Duelin's foot twitched and then was still.

Cap picked up the pistol Duelin had dropped when he fell over the railing. He checked the cylinder. "Humph. Only had one round left."

"That's enough."

Cap laid the pistol on the table. "The way I see it, you had no choice. He ventilated your coat for ya."

"Yeah, well it don't help much."

Later, Coy sat on a stump and watched as the church building smoldered. Most of the people wandered back to their beds for the rest of the night. A few men stayed, watching for spot fires from the embers that popped and streaked like meteors into the surrounding brush. Of course, with all the rain and frost they had had, it was unlikely any new fires would start.

Oh well, an ounce of prevention, as they say.

Coy took out his watch. It read twelve forty-eight. The sun would be up in another five hours. It had been a good two hours that the building had been burning. It would probably be another three or four days before it was dead out.

All that work, for what? Is God trying to tell me something? That it isn't meant to be?

When he first arrived in Rampart, he felt it was where the Lord wanted him to build a church. But now he had his doubts.

Coy looked up. Low-hanging clouds had moved in and mingled with the smoke in the still night's sub-arctic air. It absorbed the light from the fire, creating a huge orange glow above. A feeling of oppression overcame him.

"We ran out of water."

Coy turned toward the voice. Beach stood there, looking at Coy's tent.

"We did what we could, but it was too hot."

Coy had glanced at it when he sat on the stump, but the fire had held his attention. He looked more closely at the tent. The back had been scorched a dark buckskin color. There were holes in the roof from embers that had popped from the fire. Someone had collapsed the back half, evidently trying to keep it as far away from the heat as possible.

Beach gestured with his thumb toward the camp. "I'm headin' back to the cabin. Ya wanna bunk with me for the rest of the night? Ya sure look like you could use some sleep."

Coy nodded. "Thanks."

* * *

"STEEEEAM BOOOOAT!"

Coy sat upright in the bunk. Temporarily disorientated, his eyes danced around the dim interior of the cabin.

"STEEEEAM BOOOOAT!" someone yelled outside the cabin.

A melodious baritone steam whistle sounded far off.

Coy looked over at Beach, who was crawling out of his bunk.

"Evidently, there's a steamboat coming in."

Beach snickered at Coy's attempt at humor as he pulled his pants on. "Evidently. It's a big thing in these parts. Especially this time of year. It's the last chance to stock up for the long, cold, dark winter ahead and a good chance to get news from the States. Hope they have a good stock of newspapers on board."

Coy leaned over, opened the wood stove, and added a couple of wood chunks. Closing the door, he said, "Don't s'pose they'd have a ready-made church building, do ya?"

Beach stomped into his boots. "Kinda doubt that." Looking at Coy he continued, "Let's go see what they do have."

Stepping out of the cabin, Coy shrugged into his long black coat and buttoned it up, looking around as he did so.

The low-hanging clouds looked ominous, and a smell of smoke and snow filled the chilly air—air pregnant with moisture. Large cakes of pan ice swirled and jostled each other in the half-mile-wide river as they steadily floated toward the Bering Sea.

At the boat landing, the whole mining camp, it seemed, was gathering. The children chased each other playing tag, while the adults speculated on who and what was on board. The paddles slowed and the deck filled with stampeders eager to disembark as the great boat nosed into the soft silty beach.

Looking through the crowd, Coy spotted Cap Mayo working his way toward him. Beach had wandered off.

Cap stood beside Coy, looked at the boat, and shook his head. "More *cheechakoes* to babysit through the winter. Get any sleep last night?"

"Some. Bunked with Beach in his cabin."

"I didn't get a lick of sleep. Got the two bodies ready for burial. I'll go through Duelin's belongins later. See if I can find any next of kin. Chilkoot, I know didn't have any family. Except his woman, of course."

"You gonna write a report?"

Cap frowned, looked down at the ground, and then at the crowd.

"Hadn't thought of it."

"Maybe ya should. Give it to Canton so's he's aware of the details and he can forward it on to the U. S. Marshal's office in Sitka."

Cap deeply sighed. "Yeah, I guess I should. Just one more thing to add to my list."

"Well, you *are* the mayor."

Cap looked back at Coy with his piercing gray eyes and a frown on his face. "Thanks."

Turning, Cap made his way to the boat with Coy in tow.

The boat captain made his way down the steps from the wheelhouse to the main deck. As they approached, the captain called out to the crowd, "Anyone here a preacher?"

"There sure is!" someone shouted out. "He's here somewheres!"

"Here he is!" somebody close by hollered.

Everyone turned to look at Coy. He suddenly felt uncomfortable, fenced in by the crowd.

What is this all about?

23

C oy nervously worked his way through the crowd to the boat. The boat captain locked eyes with him. "You Coy Tucker, the Baptist preacher?"

"Yes sir."

"Proud to meet ya. Heard of ya, down on the Kuskokwim. Said ya walked in, pretty as ya please in Bob Duelin's saloon and made the Blueberry Kid pay back some money swindled from a miner. That true?"

Coy was surprised. "News travels fast."

The boat captain smiled. "Don't under-estimate the moccasin telegraph. Wherever stories are told around a campfire on some lonely trail at night, your name will come up. Got a load of pews for ya... Sign here," he said as he handed Coy a paper and pencil.

"I didn't order any pews."

"Didn't have to. They were donated. Some church in Seattle sent 'em up. Said to make sure they got to a Baptist preacher somewhere along the Yukon. When I heard about ya, I figured you must be the one. Besides, you're the only Baptist preacher I've found."

Coy took the paper and pencil and signed it as he spoke to Cap. "Where can I store them? I don't have a church building anymore?"

Cap scratched his beard, apparently in contemplation. Then his eyes widened.

"We can store 'em in the North Star. It's abandoned property now. And as far as I'm concerned, the North Star is yours. And no, it's not charity. You can either buy it or rent it."

Coy looked at him. *Why not?*

"Okay."

Coy handed the paper and pencil to the boat captain and shook his hand, as Cap asked for volunteers. Soon, the winches and cables groaned as the crew offloaded the cargo.

Cap leaned toward Coy to be heard over the din of the noise. "As soon as I get my stock moved up to the trading post, I'll head over to the North Star and start going through Duelin's belongins." Then he turned and walked away.

The boat captain pointed to the still-burning church building.

"What happened?"

Coy filled the captain in on what had happened during the night.

"That's a durn shame. I saw that orange glow in the distance from the wheelhouse a couple-o-hours before dawn and figured something bad had happened."

Coy watched the crowd for a while before he realized he had not seen Handshaker Bob or his shill, Camp Robber Freddy working the newcomers. Nor had he seen the Blueberry Kid, the Faro dealer, or Colorado for that matter.

That's something to think about. Are they laying low now that their boss is dead? Are they reorganizing?

Coy suddenly had an idea. Looking at the captain, he said, "I got some freight for ya. Once it's on board, you can do whatever ya want with it."

The captain gave him a quizzical look as Coy turned to leave.

Coy eased up to the North Star Saloon tent and heard subdued voices inside. Throwing back the tent flap he stepped in and faced them, feet planted firmly, shoulder-width apart. Handshaker Bob, Camp Robber Freddy and the Faro dealer were seated at a table, but the Blueberry Kid was standing.

They stared at him, wide-eyed.

"Boys! You're going on a trip and you're takin' whatever you're wearin'."

Blueberry's lip curled and he grabbed leather. Before his gun cleared the holster, Coy's pistol was leveled at his chest.

Blueberry swallowed hard and eased his pistol back down.

"Smart move, Blueberry. You keep it there and your hands away from it, and I'll let ya keep it."

Coy stepped to the side and waved his pistol toward the tent flap. "Now, let's go. Nice and easy."

The group made their way to the landing with no sudden movements that could be misinterpreted. With cheering and applause, the crowd parted before them like the Red Sea.

At the gangplank, they stopped and Handshaker Bob removed his hat. He looked at Coy and then at the captain.

"Cap'n sir, I reckon we're requestin' passage."

The boat captain looked them over. A slight grin crossed his face as he looked at Coy. Coy gave him a nod.

Looking back at the trio he asked, "Where ya headed?"

"Anywhere but here," the Blueberry Kid responded.

"Gettin' a little hot fer ya? Listen up. I'm gonna try for Fort Yukon. If I make it, I'll drop ya off there. And if ya cause any trouble, you'll be swimmin' the rest of the way. If I can't make it, I'll turn the boat around and run for St. Michael. Got that?"

"Yes sir."

The captain tossed his head toward the boat. "Climb aboard."

"Look what I found!"

Coy turned toward the voice. Cap had just entered the new North Star Saloon building, carrying a heavy chest. He grunted a little as he set it on a chair and flipped the lid open.

Coy had been cleaning up blood stains where Duelin had died. Cap's arrival was a welcome break from that gruesome task. Tossing the rag into a bucket of water, Coy walked over and peered inside. It was full of cash, gold, and jewelry. A regular pirate's trove.

"Where did ya find that?"

"We was tearin' down the old tent saloon and the boys wanted to take up the floorboards and pan out any gold dust that may have spilled through. We found this hidden under the floorboards behind the bar. They almost had a fistfight tryin' to claim it. I reckon it belongs to you since you bought the property and all."

Coy was astonished. "There must be several thousand dollars there."

"I'll say."

Coy felt a twinge of remorse and his conscience bothered him as he thought about it. The chest reminded him of the one the Buffalo Soldiers carried many years ago.

"I say, separate out the jewelry. If anyone can identify certain pieces, sight unseen, they belong to them."

"What about the cash and gold?"

"Well..." Coy began, "Wasn't there a doctor that got off the boat with the rest of 'em this morning?"

Coy's piercing gray eyes stared at Coy. "That's what I heard. Why? What's going through your brain?"

"Well, as fast as this mining camp is growin' and as dangerous as it is out on the creeks, I say that money belongs to the community. Use it to build a hospital. And a school. With the long cold winter ahead, we'll probably have a passel of youngsters come spring."

Cap shook his head as he looked around. Looking at Coy he said, "Like I said, you ain't like the others. No-siree."

Cap closed the lid, picked up the chest, and headed out the door on his way to the trader's store.

Coy finished cleaning up the blood. Tossing the red-stained water into the street, he set the pail by the door. It began snowing then, lightly. He decided he needed to bring more of his items from the tent before it got covered up down to the North Star Church.

The North Star Church? He hadn't thought of that before. It just sort of popped into his brain. Turning it over in his mind, he decided he liked it. *The one constant light. Never changing.*

Back inside, he reached for his gun belt. On second thought, he left it behind. Coy shrugged into his long black coat and stepped out into the street. Turning left, he headed to the fourth bench.

"Caleb Moore!"

Coy froze. The voice had come from behind him.

Coy slowly turned, and there stood the Colorado Kid. His coattail was pinned behind his back, giving him quick access to his *Smith and Wesson* revolver.

Coy's vision narrowed and focused on the Kid. He saw the Kid's lip twitch and grow into a half grin. Coy's hearing became acute. He heard the whispering of snowflakes as they fell. He felt every throb of his heart beating in his chest.

He saw the Kid's lips move. "I reckon it's just you and me now. Time to answer the question. Who's faster? You, or me."

Why, this one time, did I decide to not wear my guns?

"I told you once, Colorado. Caleb Moore no longer exists. I am not that person you remember."

Coy watched Colorado's eyes scrutinize him. "Well, it's true you act different. In the old days we would have been throwin' lead by now. I still wanna find out who's faster."

"What difference would it make? By the time you find out I'm faster, you'll be dead, and no one will care. If you're faster, you'll still have the camp to face. There's no place to hide in this wilderness. Especially this time of the year. And then, you'll be dead. Again, no one will care. So again, I ask, what difference would it make?"

Coy saw hesitation in the Kid's eyes. And then he saw a slight smile curl the corner of the Kid's mouth. "What's so funny?"

"Irony. That's the same thing I told Duelin."

"Well, it's true. Look, Colorado, killin' me won't raise a family. It won't get this town built. You got potential Colorado. And choices. This camp will need a good sheriff. I think you're that man."

"What happened to you Preacher? Why are you like this?"

Coy smiled and nodded toward the North Star. "Let's get off the street and I'll tell ya all about it."

END

ABOUT THE AUTHOR

As a second-generation Alaskan, Russell M. Chace was steeped in the tradition and lore of the 'Last Fronter'. Raised in a mixture of Athabascan, Inuit, and white cultures, he grew to appreciate and admire their cultures and knowledge. He learned how to pan gold on the banks of the Chatanika River from an old prospector. He spent most of his young adult life feeding his family home-grown vegetables, wild game, and fish. Much of it preserved in the old ways.

He still keeps a sourdough starter active, handed down from his mother (that she fed the family on) since the 1960s. Like his ancestors, he spent most of his young adult life wandering the ridges and valleys of the interior of Alaska—many of which appear in his books.

Russell M. Chace is the author of The Adventures of Dalton Laird series, which includes, *From Out Of The Loneliness*, *Under The Midnight Sun*, and *The Sun Dogs of Winter*.

Made in the USA
Columbia, SC
13 June 2025